Steampunk Velvet

Welcome to Steampunk Velvet, a tale of shadows, steam, and a small black cat with a very big secret.

In this charming and daring adventure set within the greater Jedidiah Davenport universe, we follow Velvet—a sleek, clever feline who's far more than she seems. Equal parts spy, stowaway, and silent observer, Velvet prowls the edges of human conflict and invention with quiet confidence and a sharp set of claws.

This is a story of unlikely heroes: a cat in a leather vest, her adopted brother and sister, a mouse with courage far bigger than his size, and a tomcat with a top hat and a past of his own. Together, they uncover plots, sneak through airships, and face down enemies far larger than themselves—because sometimes, it takes the smallest voices to speak the loudest truths.

Steampunk Velvet is a whimsical yet thrilling addition to the Davenport saga, weaving through the events of both Sky Races and Quest for the Lost Relic, while offering its own tale of loyalty, mystery, and mechanical mischief. Expect daring escapes, whispered secrets, electrified feathers—and heart. Lots of heart.

Whether you're a devoted fan of the Jedidiah Davenport series or stepping into this steampunk world for the first time, Velvet's story is sure to whisk you away on an unforgettable journey.

The Steampunk Velvet series is dedicated to all the real-life animals who inspired their fictional counterparts—Velvet, Dottie, Panther, Alex, Saber, Rustina, and Fuzzy Face (aka Princess Bonita).

So perch somewhere cozy, flick your tail, and prepare to prowl the foggy rooftops of London and beyond.

Velvet's story is just getting started.

Velvet darted through the shadows,
weaving between trees and shrubs, but
the mechanical bird followed close behind.

Steampunk Velvet

A Victorian Cat and her Amazing Adventures

BY PAUL EDWARD TURNER

Copyright Notice

Steampunk Velvet a novel by Paul Edward Turner

© 2025 Paul Edward Turner

ISBN 979-8-9924477-4-3 (paperback)

www.pauledwardturner.com

Cover Design by: Paul Edward Turner

First Edition: July 29th, 2025

Contents

CHAPTER I

Top Hats and Tails

It was a warm summer evening in New York City, on July 15th, 1881, and the back alley behind Whitmore's Bookshop was draped in shadows. The air was thick with the kind of summer heat that made the brick walls sweat, but a certain little black cat with a white patch on her chest didn't seem to mind.

She was too busy enjoying her dinner.

A small saucer of leftover stew had been set out by the back door, still warm. Mr. Whitmore had a habit of feeding strays. He claimed it kept the rats away and brought good luck. The little cat lapped at the broth with cautious appreciation, occasionally pausing to glance over her shoulder.

That's when she spotted them.

Two tall figures standing at the far end of the alley, half-silhouetted in hazy gaslight. They wore long, dark coats and wide-brimmed hats, and smooth, curved plague masks that completely obscured their faces. Even though they didn't carry weapons, there was something unsettling about the way they silently watched her.

One of them lifted a gloved hand and pointed.

Out of instinct, the little cat's ears flattened. Her muscles tensed, and then she ran.

The little white patch on her chest heaved up and down. Her tail puffed and rigid as she raced down the alley. It was dim, narrow, and slick from an earlier rain, but she could clearly see them chasing behind her.

The two figures moved in unnerving silence. Their long coats brushed the cobblestones as they continued in pursuit.

She turned and bolted down another alley.

Boots continued to strike the pavement behind her—slow, deliberate steps with no rush in them. As if they already knew the chase would end in their favor.

She darted beneath a rickety cart, then sprang up a stack of crates. Her claws dug into rotting wood as she scrambled for the fire escape above.

Behind her, the soft scuff of boots never quickened. The figures weren't rushing, weren't shouting. They moved—silent and certain—as though they knew exactly where she was going to run next.

She judged the distance and leaped onto the

lowest rung. From there she clambered to the iron platform above. Her small body pressed against the warm metal as she paused, ears twitching, trying to decide if they had followed.

Nothing.

Then a low creak.

She turned her head just in time to see one of the masked figures stepping onto the crate below, reaching upward.

She hissed again and started climbing higher until she was on the top fire escape. She raced to the edge, leaping to a nearby windowsill, and then to a sloped rooftop of a shorter building beside her. She didn't dare look back.

For a moment, the night opened up in front of her—a patchwork of tarred shingles and narrow ledges, laundry lines swaying between buildings, chimneys puffing out coils of steam. If she could just make it far enough, fast enough, maybe she could lose them in the maze of the city.

But she only made it across a few more rooftops before something wrapped around her hind legs. It was a thin and wiry net.

"Oh no. No, no, no—" she hissed, biting into it.

This net buzzed with a faint hum—like static in the air before a thunderstorm. It didn't shock her, but it clung to her, tightening more and more as she tried to twist free.

She thrashed against it and repeatedly shouted,

"Put me down!"

But all the masked figures heard was a series of agitated meows and hisses.

The black cat continued kicking and thrashing as the world began to spin around her. A second later, she was lifted—gently, but firmly—into the arms of one of the masked figures. The other produced a small cloth sack, opened it, and with one quick motion, they slipped her inside.

That's when everything went dark and very, very quiet.

****

Three weeks later and several thousand feet in the air...

The little black cat blinked her eyes as she began to wake up. She placed a paw over her face shielding herself from the golden light filtering through a set of lace curtains. Beyond the glass, clouds drifted past in a slow swirl, giving the strange, dizzying sense that the world itself was moving. Somewhere nearby, a grandfather clock chimed eight in the morning with crisp, deliberate notes. The scent of lavender and wood smoke hung in the air—a scent she had grown very familiar with.

She was lying on a red satin cushion near a tall window, draped in fabric so expensive it made her whiskers twitch.

She stretched, rolled onto her side... and then froze. She had woken up on this pillow many times now but this time, something was different.

Something was on her.

She was wearing a custom black leather vest. Her tail lashed in alarm, and as she sat up, a pair of tiny brass goggles slipped forward and dangled around her neck. She pawed at them, annoyed.

That's when she noticed a top hat delicately perched between her ears like the world's most ridiculous crown.

"You've got to be kidding," she hissed. "She's got me made up like a circus clown."

From across the room, a calm voice spoke. "Come now, Velvet. You've been aboard my ship for almost a month now. It's high time you began looking like you belong to me."

Ever since the night of her capture, Velvet had been the guest aboard an airship known as the Aetherwind. This veritable floating palace belonged to none other than Lady Seraphina Blackwood.

The small black cat turned.

The aristocratic woman stood near a grand oak drafting table, the morning sun haloing her silhouette. Her presence commanded the room—dressed in a high-collared, dark velvet gown adorned with ornate metalwork and decorative buttons that caught the light like polished brass. A wide belt wrapped around her waist, fastened with intricate clasps, and her long cape trailed behind her like ink in water. Her dark hair was styled into a smooth twist, and her sharp green eyes missed nothing.

The little cat gave a low growl and shook her head, trying to knock the hat off her head. To her great annoyance, it stayed put.

"You were a mess when my guards picked you up and brought you in," Seraphina stated, unfurling a scroll covered in mechanical diagrams. "But I knew you had potential. The perfect feline version of... well of me, of course."

The cat opened her mouth to protest—but only a raspy, indignant *mrrrow* came out.

Lady Blackwood chuckled faintly without looking up. "In time you'll get used to those clothes. Maybe even grow to like them."

The little black cat jumped down from the cushion with a soft thump, trotted across the polished hardwood floor, and hopped up onto a nearby vanity.

She blinked at her reflection in the mirror.

The vest fit rather well. Sleek, tailored, and surprisingly comfortable. The goggles still felt a bit heavy, but they gleamed in the light like polished brass buttons. And the top hat... well, the top hat was ridiculous. But she tilted her head slightly,

Velvet hopped onto the vanity and
blinked at her reflection in the mirror.

watching it tip at just the right angle.

She didn't hate it.

But.

She couldn't let Seraphina know that. So, she raised a paw and hissed at her own reflection.

After, she turned away from the mirror and leaped from the vanity to the floor. She padded across the room and leaped up onto the drafting table. Her paws landed with the grace of someone who'd done it a hundred times.

Lady Blackwood's scroll was unfurled across the surface, secured by tiny brass weights at each corner. It was covered in strange symbols, concentric circles, and finely drawn mechanisms that evoked a deep sense of mystery. The cat narrowed her eyes, studying the lines and notations like she understood more than she let on.

"Off," Seraphina said flatly, brushing her away with the back of her hand.

Velvet didn't budge.

Lady Blackwood let out a slow breath. "Are you that curious to know what this is?" She turned toward the cat annoyed. "This, my little fur ball, is the schematics for something far beyond your comprehension. It's a device known by the name of the Chronomechanism."

She picked up a metal rod and tapped on one of the drawings near its center. "The most advanced and delicate piece of temporal engineering ever conceived. Not that you'd understand, of course."

The little black cat cocked her head, tail curling thoughtfully.

Seraphina didn't notice. She had already returned her focus to the schematics.

For a moment, all was silent.

Suddenly, a knock at the door disrupted the quiet.

One of the masked guards stepped into the room, moving with the same eerie calm as always.

Out of instinct, Velvet leaped from the drafting table and hid under the ornate bed nearby.

The guard held a sealed envelope between his gloved fingers and offered it to Lady Blackwood without a word.

She took it with a nod. The wax seal was marked with a sigil—an octopus wearing a monocle and a top hat.

Velvet's ears perked at the subtle snap of the wax being broken.

Seraphina unfolded the letter, her eyes scanning the page with measured interest. "Ah," she said under her breath. "The final roster!"

The little cat narrowed her eyes and crept a little closer, peeking out from under the bed skirt, straining to see what was happening.

"These are the confirmed contestants for the Sky Races," Lady Blackwood murmured, mostly to herself. "Let's hope they prove to be as resourceful as they are financially endowed. Whoever wins that race will be securing their place in history forever."

Her nose crinkled slightly as she read one of the names on the paper.

"Jedidiah Davenport?" Seraphina muttered, puzzled. "I don't remember seeing that name on any of the social registers." She turned toward the guard. "Find out everything you can on this newcomer. If the Order doesn't have a file on him, start one!"

The little cat tilted her head, curious.

The aristocratic woman suddenly looked outraged as her eyes fell on another name.

"Professor Thaddeus Montgomery!" Seraphina shouted, her voice sharp enough to make the little cat leap for cover. "What does he think he's doing entering my race?"

"As if I didn't have enough to deal with staying one step ahead of the Clockwork Conqueror!"

In one fluid motion, she grabbed a letter opener from her desk and flung it across the room. The blade stuck fast in a wanted poster tacked to the far wall—right between the goggles of a man wearing a brass-plated mask.

Velvet flinched.

"Come with me," Seraphina muttered, adjusting her gloves as she turned on her heel and stormed out of the room, the guard right behind her.

Velvet crawled out from under the bed and

leaped back onto the drafting table.

The blueprint was still spread open.

She crept forward and sat down next to it. Her whiskers twitched as she sniffed it. It didn't make sense—yet it fascinated her.

She reached out a paw and gently tapped one of the tiny brass weights, nudging it slightly.

She gave a low, thoughtful *mrrp*, then tapped one claw against the edge of the paper.

Just then, something caught her eye.

A symbol had been lightly sketched onto the corner of the paper—faint, nearly invisible unless the parchment was lifted. Velvet pressed her nose against the weight and gave it another nudge.

There it was.

An octopus with a monocle and top hat, just like the wax seal.

Velvet blinked.

Before she could paw at it again, a sound came from the hallway—fast, sharp footsteps returning.

She jumped down from the table and darted behind the curtain just as the door reopened.

"I'm not backing this race just for that oaf to enter and make a mockery out of everything I'm trying to do!" Lady Seraphina fumed, striding back into the room.

The masked guard followed silently behind her, unreadable as ever.

Seraphina snatched the letter from the edge of

the table, waving it in the air. "I hope he knows what he's up to!" she snapped. "The entire Order must be laughing at me for letting this slip my attention!"

From behind the curtain, the little black cat blinked slowly, her ears twitching.

"Something about those guards in the bird masks has never smelled right," she muttered, wrinkling her nose and baring her teeth like she'd caught a whiff of something foul.

Velvet didn't know what they were planning, or what a Sky Race was, but something seemed odd to her. And whatever happened next, she intended to be ready.

****

Almost six weeks later, on Saturday, September 17th, 1881...

From the rusted rooftop of an abandoned grain silo on the outskirts of Wichita, six silent figures watched the airfield where hundreds of people had gathered to see the end of the Sky Race.

Lady Seraphina Blackwood stood near the edge, her velvet cloak fluttering gently in the late summer breeze. Beside her, four plague-masked guards remained motionless—hooded, still, and ever watchful. No one below noticed them. The townsfolk were too busy cheering, their voices rising like cannonfire as the airship race reached its final moments.

The finish line was a blur of banners, brass instruments, and waving handkerchiefs. Fireworks popped in the sky. Onlookers climbed barrels and crates just to get a better view. And overhead, like silver arrows slicing the air, the airships closed in.

Velvet crouched at the edge of the rooftop, her tail flicking. Her brass goggles, now resting on the brim of her top hat, reflected the sky as she squinted upward, following the ships.

Seraphina stood still as stone.

Then came the roar.

The crowd erupted in cheers so loud they shook the silo beneath them. The race was over.

Seraphina's lips tightened. "And that's how it ended."

Velvet tilted her head. She couldn't quite read Seraphina's tone. Disappointment? Satisfaction? A mix of both?

The woman turned, her voice calm but cold. "We'll need to make preparations."

Behind her, one of the guards gave a subtle nod.

Velvet remained at the rooftop's edge a moment longer, eyes scanning the celebration below. She didn't know who had won. But she knew, instinctively, that something had changed.

Then she turned and followed the others.

****

About two weeks later on October 4th, 1881...

Deep in the Kansas plains, in a town called Spoon Fork, the morning sun bathed the dusty streets in a golden light, casting long shadows over the bustling train station. Banners fluttered from every post, and a brass band played cheerful tunes near the entrance, trying in vain to rise above the clamor of the crowd.

Hidden among the rooftops overlooking the grand opening, Velvet lay low behind a chimney stack. Her brass goggles neatly perched on her top hat, and her tail twitched with anticipation. It had taken her months of subtle observation and patience to plan something she had dreamed of since the day she had first been captured, and today was her chance to finally achieve this goal.

Below, the four plague-masked guards stood near the edge of the platform, eyes sweeping the crowd with quiet vigilance. Lady Seraphina Blackwood stood among them, her dark attire stark against the cheerful backdrop of the festivities. She wasn't mingling. She wasn't speaking. She was waiting.

Velvet had slipped away while they were distracted.

She padded along the rooftop, surveying the

sprawling scene below. The train was a magnificent thing—long, emerald green, trimmed in gold, with steam hissing from its joints and sunlight glinting off its polished surfaces. Dozens of people were crowded onto the platform, their full and undivided attention fixed on the president of the railroad.

With a soft *mrrp*, Velvet crept down the rusted ladder of the telegraph office nearby. She slid down a loose shutter and darted through the alley behind the general store, then disappeared into the crowd.

No one noticed her.

She weaved between boots and skirts, tail low, moving with a practiced ease. Seraphina's voice— sharp and disapproving—drifted faintly over the noise, but Velvet didn't look back. Her paws struck the wooden platform just as the final speech concluded and the conductor bellowed, "All aboard!"

A cheer went up. It was the perfect distraction.

Velvet slipped beneath a bench then darted toward the train. With a quick bound, she slipped through the half-open door of the baggage car. Inside, crates and trunks lined the walls in haphazard stacks. She crept behind a battered steamer trunk and froze—silent, invisible.

Minutes later, the train lurched forward and started its journey. She didn't know where she was going—and frankly, she didn't care. She was free.

CHAPTER II

The Cat Farm

Later that night, as the rhythmic clatter of the train was lulling most of the passengers asleep, Velvet was nestled in the corner of the baggage car between two leather satchels that she had used to sharpen her claws on. She lay curled up on a heavy wool coat that she had managed to pull down from an overhead rack. It smelled faintly of pipe tobacco and leather polish. The hum of the steam engine, the sway of the car, and the occasional muffled voice drifted around her like a lullaby. But the little black cat wasn't dozing. On the contrary, she was wide awake, calculating her next move.

Somewhere not far beyond the walls of the train, the Kansas plains rolled past under a silver-washed sky. The moon, high and watchful, shined down on the train as it chugged eastward—toward St. Louis.

A sudden hiss of steam jolted the quiet. The

train gave a low groan and gradually began to slow.

Velvet rose, stretched once, and began sniffing the air. Outside the windows, lanterns flickered to life at a small outpost—a water tower, nothing more.

The train hissed again as it rolled to a halt beside the tower, steam curling around the wheels. Crew members jumped down from the cars to refill the boiler.

Velvet's ears perked.

This was her moment.

With nimble precision, she slipped from between the baggage, sharpening her claws one last time. The door at the rear of the baggage car was cracked open, allowing a breeze to enter. She padded toward it without a sound.

A man with a lantern passed by on the platform outside but didn't glance her way. A porter yawned and adjusted his cap. The side door of the baggage car had also been left open. Velvet slipped through it and dropped to the ground with barely a sound.

She landed softly in the thick grass and immediately darted beneath a low platform, crouching there as the hiss of water poured into the boiler above.

No one saw her. No one called out.

Velvet glanced up at the train's windows, watching the glow of lanterns flicker past. Inside, a few conversations continued.

She gave a small, smug trill to herself.

And then she turned, disappearing into the tall prairie grass with only the moon to see her go.

Velvet hid far out of sight as the train groaned to life and began its journey eastward without her. She watched its last car as it vanished into the dark of night, a distant whistle echoing faintly behind it.

She moved on.

The Kansas plains were vast and unfamiliar. By day, the sun was unrelenting, and by night, the silence was heavy, save for the occasional rustle in the grass or call of a distant coyote. Velvet kept low, moving from shadow to shadow, always alert.

By the third day, the thrill of escape had given way to something more gnawing.

Hunger.

She had gone too long without a proper meal. She nosed around dry bushes, stared longingly at distant farmhouses, and even considered pawing at a kitchen door once—but the barking of a dog made her rethink that plan.

Then came the rain.

It began with a soft drizzle, but within minutes, it turned into a full downpour. The dry earth turned to mud beneath her paws. Thunder rumbled across the open fields like a sky-born train, and the wind howled through the tall grass.

Velvet darted for the nearest cover she could find—an old, weather-beaten wagon half-sunken into the earth beside a forgotten stretch of fence.

She squeezed beneath it, water dripping steadily through the broken slats above. Her vest was soaked, her goggles fogged, and her top hat was beginning to lose its shape.

She curled up tightly and shivered, her ears flicking at every clap of thunder.

So much for freedom.

She gave a low, tired *mrrp*.

The world had grown bigger than she expected. And far lonelier.

A jagged flash of lightning lit up the landscape like a photograph. For the briefest moment, Velvet saw it—a house, not far beyond the wagon. Its windows glowed warm and golden through the rain, and smoke curled gently from a crooked chimney. There was something inviting about it. Lopsided shutters. A porch swing that creaked with the wind. It wasn't grand, but it looked... kind.

Velvet blinked the rain from her eyes.

She began to think back to Mr. Whitmore's bookshop back in New York. What a kind man he was and how he used to keep her fed.

Maybe this house had someone like that too.

She crouched low and sprinted across the open field, the rain soaking her completely in a matter of seconds. The wind bit at her ears, but she didn't stop. Her little paws splashed through puddles and slipped on muddy roots, but the porch was getting closer.

A second flash lit the world up again—closer this time—and Velvet leaped onto the front step just as thunder cracked overhead. She crouched against the wooden boards, dripping, shivering, and panting.

Then she raised both front paws and started scratching on the door.

A moment passed.

Then another.

Velvet gave a plaintive *mrrrow*.

Inside, she heard the creak of a chair, followed by slow footsteps coming near. The door creaked open, spilling yellow lamplight across the boards.

A tall man loomed in the doorway, lantern in hand. He was lanky and stoop-shouldered, with a drooping mustache and the unmistakable scent of other cats clinging to him like a second skin. His eyes narrowed beneath the brim of his hat as he looked down.

Velvet stood there, soaked and trembling.

She took one step across the threshold—then collapsed.

Her legs gave out. She slumped against the open door and slid to the floor with a faint, exhausted sigh. Her little top hat landing on the floor beside her.

Velvet slumped against the open door and
slid to the floor with a faint, exhausted sigh.
Her little top hat landing on the floor beside her.

****

The next morning, Velvet woke to the faint scent of woodsmoke and something warm beneath her. The ache in her limbs had dulled, replaced by a heavy sleepiness that clung like cobwebs. She stirred, blinking her eyes, and yawned.

That's when it hit her, she wasn't outside anymore.

Instead, she found herself nestled on a folded wool blanket near a cast-iron stove. A kettle whistled softly in the background, and morning light filtered through dusty windows. The storm was gone. In its place was a quiet, creaky warmth.

And two sets of green eyes staring at her.

Velvet's ears flattened. She shot up with a startled hiss, back arched and fur bristling. The blanket tumbled off her as she stood her ground, tail puffed like a bottlebrush.

The two cats watching her scrambled back a few steps in alarm.

They were both black like her—though not quite the same. The younger of the two was taller and slimmer, his coat sleek and neat, and his green eyes sparkled with mischief. The other was stockier, with a rounder face and a bobbed tail that twitched nervously behind her. She also had a patch of white fur on her chest like Velvet.

The slim one looked at the bob-tailed one and said dryly, "You lost, Dottie. She did make it through the night."

Velvet blinked, still panting.

Dottie sighed. "She looked like she wasn't going to!"

"Well, she did," the tall one replied, sitting down with a swish of his tail. "So that means you owe me your share of breakfast."

"You already ate it!"

"Oh yeah, I forgot."

Velvet's eyes darted between the two of them, unsure whether to keep hissing or collapse again.

Dottie took a hesitant step forward. "Are you okay?"

"Who are you and where am I?" Velvet hissed defensively.

The taller cat tilted his head. "Name's Panther," he said, casually. "That one with the tail issue is Dottie. You're in the home of Hiram Pike."

"Hiram Pike?" Velvet meowed confused.

"He takes in stray cats," Dottie explained. "He takes good care of us until he finds us new homes."

"Just don't sharpen your claws on his boots," Panther quickly added. "Or knock over his jars, and definitely don't sit on his paperwork."

Velvet didn't answer. Not right away. She simply stared at them, still tense, still ready to bolt —but slowly, her breathing began to settle.

She was still here.

Still alive.

And, for the first time in days, not on the run.

Suddenly, Velvet's ears twitched.

Something wasn't right.

Her gaze dropped suddenly to her chest—and her fur fluffed in alarm.

Her vest was gone.

She rolled her eyes back and tilted her head up. Her top hat and brass goggles were missing too.

She looked down at herself in a panic, then back up at the two cats. "Where are they?" she hissed, voice sharp and accusatory.

Panther blinked. "Where's what?"

"My clothes!" she growled, stepping forward. "Where are my vest, my goggles, and my hat?!"

Dottie's ears flattened. "We didn't take them!"

"Liar," Velvet spat, narrowing her eyes. "You took them from me while I was asleep!"

Panther raised his voice. "Whoa now. We wouldn't take your things. It wasn't us. It was him."

"Who—?"

"Hiram Pike," Panther said turning toward the doorway into the parlor. "He took them off you last night. They were soaked. He hung them up somewhere to dry."

As if on cue, a distant creak echoed across the floorboards. Somewhere deeper in the house, the metallic clink of a lantern being adjusted rang out, followed by a low, gravelly cough.

Velvet froze.

Her eyes darted toward the hallway, her tail flicking low. She hadn't forgotten the man who answered the door—the looming figure with the grass-stained boots and quiet stare.

"He didn't hurt you," Dottie said quickly.

"You said he takes in strays?" Velvet sniffed the air. "I smell more cats than just the three of us.

"They're outside. Keeps most of us out in the barn till someone comes by needing a mouser."

"Farmers mostly," Panther added, hopping on the counter and looking out the window. "They'll either trade a sack of grain or a few coins, sometimes eggs, and boom—off you go to chase mice."

He kept staring out the window. "Come see for yourself."

Velvet joined him hesitantly, her paws silent on the wooden floor.

Beyond the glass, the early morning sun was just starting to burn away the last of the mist. And across a patch of worn grass and old fence posts, stood a weathered barn. Its side doors hung open, and inside, Velvet saw movement—tails flicking, ears twitching, dozens of cats lounging on bales of hay or pacing between feed bins.

Some watched birds through gaps in the wall. Others slept in clusters. All of them… waiting.

"He only keeps a few of us in the house," Panther murmured.

"To make sure his place stays mice-free," Dottie added.

Velvet stared out at the barn, silent.

Then, quietly, she said, "He better not have bent my hat or soiled my vest."

Despite all her earlier protests about the clown costume as she originally called it, Velvet had grown accustomed to wearing them.

Panther hopped off the counter just as the sound of footsteps creaked across the floorboards behind them.

Velvet turned sharply.

Hiram Pike stepped into the kitchen. He picked Velvet up and gently placed her on the floor.

"No cats on the counter!" He stated firmly.

After that, he took out a chipped ceramic bowl in one hand a ladle in the other, and dipped out something from a pot on the stove.

Steam rose in lazy curls from the stew he dumped in the bowl. Rich chunks of meat, a few vegetables, and the unmistakable scent of something hearty and homemade.

He didn't say a word. Just crouched down near the stove and set the bowl gently on the floor a few feet from her. His face remained unreadable beneath the brim of his old hat, the lines around his eyes deep but not unkind. Then, with a quiet grunt, he stood and walked away, vanishing into the next room.

Velvet narrowed her eyes, her nose twitching. She padded closer, cautiously at first, sniffing it with a faint wrinkle of her brow.

Panther leaned in. "It's good. Trust me. I'll eat it if you don't want it..."

Velvet glanced over at him, then back to the stew.

After a moment's hesitation, hunger won.

She dove in.

The warmth hit her tongue like a lightning bolt of comfort. She lapped up the meal with barely a pause, not even bothering to look up until the bowl was nearly empty. Her whiskers dripped with broth and her sides rose and fell in steady, satisfied breaths.

She sat back, licking her paw once, then looked toward the door where Hiram had disappeared.

"Thank you," she said softly, tail curling.

But of course, all Hiram heard in the next room was a grateful *mrrrow*.

"This would be so much easier if only humans could understand what we said," Velvet remarked as she began to bathe herself.

Dottie agreed. "Unfortunately they just don't seem to be that smart."

****

Almost two weeks later Velvet was still residing at the Pike cat farm. She had decided, somewhat reluctantly at first, that this wasn't the worst place on earth and that she might as well stay a while.

After all, she had a warm dry corner of the parlor all to herself, fresh stew, and a window ledge that caught the best afternoon sun. Her vest, goggles, and top hat had been returned long ago, freshly brushed and none the worse for wear. She kept them stacked neatly beside her favorite sleeping spot—though she frequently made a point to ensure that Panther and Dottie hadn't touched them.

Most days had passed in a sleepy rhythm. Panther spent his time pretending not to care about anything and Dottie practiced her pouncing in the hallway, knocking over the same boot three times before Hiram finally gave up and moved it.

Velvet had grown used to the sounds of the place—the clink of jars, the creak of barn doors, and the occasional muttered uttering from Hiram when a stubborn latch refused to cooperate.

On the morning of October 20th, 1881, Velvet sat on the windowsill with her goggles pulled down over her eyes. Outside, a customer had just arrived —a stocky woman with a straw hat and a dust-covered wagon. Velvet watched as Hiram led her to the barn, the woman pointing toward one of the younger cats lounging in the loft.

And with that one gesture, another mouser was adopted.

"You know," Velvet said aloud to no one in particular, "this isn't such a bad little operation. If I ran it, there's a few things I'd do differently. But still."

Panther yawned from his place on the rug. "You planning to take over?"

"I just might," Velvet shot back. "So keep that in mind next time you feel like knocking over my water bowl!"

Dottie peeked in from the kitchen doorway, whiskers twitching. "You think we're getting tuna today?"

"Doubt it," Panther muttered. "Today smells like Thursday. We always have fish stew on Thursdays."

Velvet narrowed her eyes. "You've memorized the food schedule?"

"I have priorities."

Velvet shook her head and turned back to the window, tail twitching thoughtfully.

But as the sun climbed higher, something in the wind shifted. A scent... or maybe just a feeling. Faint, but not unfamiliar. A memory of smoke, brass, and leather. Something that didn't belong out here on the prairie.

She narrowed her eyes.

Someone was coming.

She sniffed the air and tilted her head.

Panther squinted at her. "You smell something odd?"

Just then, a distant creak echoed from outside. A covered supply wagon rattled into the yard, pulled by a spry-looking young horse. At the reins sat a man with a lopsided derby hat, a crooked grin, and a battered satchel resting beside him.

He wore suspenders that had lost their elasticity, a faded checkered shirt, and boots that looked older than him. But his eyes sparkled with a mix of curiosity and mischief.

He dismounted with a grunt and waved lazily at Hiram, who was already shuffling off the porch with his arms crossed.

"Mornin'!" He called out cheerfully. "I hear you're the man to see if a fella's got a mice problem and no cat to solve it."

Hiram said nothing at first. Then he nodded once and gestured toward the barn.

"So, that's where you keep them." The rotund man tipped his hat back. "I'm lookin' to take back two or three good cats. Need em' to be good with mice but easy on the furniture."

He scratched his chin. "And they gotta get along with a cook who sings off key, while he's baking pies."

Velvet narrowed her eyes.

Panther gasped. "Did he say pies?"

Dottie groaned. "He's got Panther's attention."

Velvet crept a little closer to the open window, tail twitching. She didn't know what he wanted. But he wasn't like other humans.

Something that felt oddly familiar.

"I've got just what you're looking for mister!" Hiram Pike announced as he turned on his heel and started walking.

The heavy-set man followed Hiram into the barn, his boots squelching slightly in the soft earth. Velvet and the others watched from the window, ears perked as the two men disappeared into the shadows.

Inside, muffled conversation drifted back to the house—mostly the heavy-set man's voice, curious and animated.

"Mm-hmm. Yep. Lotta tails. Don't know about that one though."

Pause.

"This one won't do either."

Pause.

"Cute batch, don't get me wrong, but I'm lookin' for something… special. See, my name's Pat Bennington. These cats are for Davenport Ranch and it's one of the most interesting places around. Its got folks who fly around in airships and talk to clocks."

Hiram muttered something in response. Velvet couldn't make it out.

Another pause.

"No, no—I'm not tryin' to be picky, but I need some trained cats. Or at least that has been housebroken. Got anything like that?"

There was a long silence.

Then the creak of the barn doors again as Hiram stepped back out into the light. Pat followed, still chatting with his hands.

"I mean, I ain't askin' for a miracle, just a couple cats who know where to do their business and where not to. That's all."

Hiram gave a grunt and motioned for him to follow.

Back in the kitchen, Panther let out a groan. "Aw no. He's bringing him in here."

Velvet stood a little taller. "Why?"

"Because he wants special cats" Dottie muttered, "we're house cats. That makes the three of us special."

Panther gasped. "What if he picks me?"

"Impossible." Dottie yawned.

"How come?"

"You're not housebroken."

"Oh yeah..." Panther suddenly whirled his head and hissed, "I am too!"

Suddenly, the front door creaked open. Heavy

boots stepped onto the floorboards.

Pat sniffed the air. "Ooo smells like stew in here. You makin' lunch?"

Hiram ignored him and gestured broadly toward the three cats peeking their heads into the room.

"Gosh," Pat said, crouching a little. "Now these critters look interesting."

His eyes flicked from Panther to Dottie and finally landed on Velvet.

Velvet's fur bristled slightly.

"She's wearing goggles," Pat said, sounding concerned. "She ain't got any trouble seeing does she?"

Hiram grunted. "She just likes wearing them."

"Uh-huh." Pat tilted his head. "Well, well... you three look like a regular little gang. The real question is are y'all mousers or mischief-makers?"

Panther sat up straighter. "Mischief-makers," he said proudly—though all Hiram heard was a short *mrrrow*.

Pat chuckled.

Velvet looked the stranger over carefully. Something about him felt odd.

The newcomer dusted some crumbs from his beard and asked, "How much do you want for all three of them?"

Hiram Pike hesitated for a moment and said, "Well, I..."

"I don't suppose," Pat began, glancing up at the

man, "three fine cats like these come cheap."

He reached into his shirt and produced a wad of folded bills from his pocket. "What do you want for the lot? Three dollars? Five?"

Hiram scratched at the side of his face, eyes lingering on the trio. "Three... no... five... no... how much do you have?"

"They're house-trained?" Pat asked, cocking an eyebrow. "They keep mice away?"

Hiram nodded. "Don't scratch nothin'. Never had a single mouse stick its head inside the house."

"I'll take 'em," Pat muttered, counting out the bills. "Five dollars sounds like a good price."

"Each!" The lanky man spoke up.

"Well, I don't know..."

Velvet gave him a long look. Panther flicked his tail.

Dottie leaned in and whispered, "Are we okay with this?"

"Depends," Panther shrugged. "Does the human make good stew?"

"Are you kidding? I make great stew!" Pat turned and looked right at Panther. "Ask anybody in Spoon Fork and they'll tell you I make the best stew this side of Wichita!"

All three cats immediately turned and looked at the rotund man.

Velvet let her goggles drop off her face as she asked, "Did you just understand what he said?"

Pat turned his gaze toward her.

"Of course I did," he chuckled. "Doesn't everybody?"

CHAPTER III

The Man Who Spoke Cat

All three cats stared at the rotund man.

Velvet's green eyes narrowed. "Say that again," she said in a tone that Pat Bennington heard as words and Hiram Pike heard as meows.

"Which part?" Pat blinked. "The part about understanding what he said or the part about me making the best stew this side of Wichita!"

Panther gasped, stepping forward. "He did it again!"

Dottie's mouth hung open. "You really can understand us, can't you?"

"Well sure," Pat said with a casual shrug, as he kneeled down beside them. "Been doing it all my life. Ain't that unusual is it?"

Velvet's jaw nearly dropped. "Yes! It's very unusual!"

"Ah," Pat said, scratching the back of his neck. "Well... I reckon I never thought much about it.

Pat kneeled down beside the three cats
and continued his conversation with them.

Always figured animals just talked to folks who knew how to listen."

"Say, fellow," Hiram suddenly spoke up, only hearing Pat's side of the conversation. "Where'd you say you escaped from?"

"Escaped?" The heavy-set man turned and faced the other human. "Something wrong with you, mister? I said I was from Davenport Ranch!"

"And did your room at this..." Hiram thought for a moment before saying "Ranch..." Then he quickly asked, "Did it have padded walls?"

"Mister, you ain't touched in the head, are you?" Pat turned and shot a glance at the three cats. "He's a strange fellow, ain't he?"

Panther moved closer to Dottie and whispered, "I don't know where this human came from, but I like him."

"Me too!" Dottie meowed.

Velvet slowly paced a circle around Pat, her tail flicking thoughtfully. "If you can understand me, then you'd better listen closely. I am not some barn cat. I am not a house pet. I was the personal feline of..." She suddenly stopped herself realizing it might be better not to reveal who she used to belong to.

"Of who?" Pat asked curiously.

"Someone very important." Velvet sat down properly and wrapped her tail around her feet.

"Ohhh," Pat nodded as if that explained

everything. "Well, I reckon you're used to eating high on the hog."

"Yes," Velvet snapped. "I'm a very special cat. Around certain circles, I'm known by the name of Steampunk Velvet."

"Who calls you that?" Panther asked innocently, only for Dottie to boop him on the nose and make him take a step back.

Pat blinked, then broke into a huge smile. "You three are gonna fit right in at the ranch."

Velvet tilted her head to the side. "Excuse me?"

"I mean," Pat continued, already turning back to Hiram, "we got airships, robots, clocks that explode, a guy who talks like a thesaurus—what's a few talking cats gonna hurt?"

"Well I don't know," Hiram Pike was hesitant to sell his three prized felines to a man claiming to be able to have a full conversation with them. "You sure you're allowed to have pets where you come from?"

Pat Bennington replied by holding up three five-dollar silver certificates.

"Do you need me to load them in your wagon for you?" Hiram asked as he snatched the bills from Pat's hand and stuck them in his pocket before the rotund man could change his mind.

****

A few hours later the wagon Pat Bennington arrived in rattled down the dusty road with a steady rhythm, the prairie sun beginning to dip low behind them. Velvet sat perched proudly on the wooden bench beside the bearded man, once again wearing her black leather vest, while her brass goggles rested atop the brim of her little top hat. The wind tugged gently at her fur, but she sat unbothered—dignified and silent.

Dottie and Panther lounged on either side of her, taking in the scenery with lazy curiosity.

Pat chuckled to himself as he gave the reins a casual flick. "You shoulda seen the fellow's face when I told him you wanted your vest and hat because you were taking them with you."

"He couldn't figure out how you even knew about them," Panther muttered, starting to bathe himself.

"Wasn't leaving without them," Velvet replied, flicking her tail pridefully. "Do you have any idea how hard it is to find clothes in my size, let alone goggles?"

"I still don't know how you see through those things," Dottie whispered, leaning in to take a sniff.

"It's more about how I look in them not how I look through them," Velvet answered flatly.

Pat let out another chuckle and leaned back a little on the bench. "You little critters are somethin' else. The folks at Davenport Ranch ain't gonna know what hit them."

As the wagon crested a small hill, the gates of the ranch came into view—a broad stretch of fenced-in land dotted with workshops, bunkhouses, and the towering silhouette of the Victorian manor. The wind carried the faint smell of smoke, metal, and something sweet cooking in a distant pot.

"Well, here we are." The rotund man announced as he reined the wagon to a stop. "This is where I work. And pretty soon, the three of you will be as well."

Velvet, Panther, and Dottie all three narrowed their eyes at the horizon.

"Now, before we head in," Pat muttered, tipping his hat back, "lemme give you the lay of the land."

"That big house down there belongs to Jedidiah Davenport. Real nice fella. He's an inventor, explorer, and business tycoon. He owns the biggest freight company in this part of the country."

"Inside the house, you'll meet my best friend and coworker Agatha Porter. You can call her Aggy. She really likes that. She runs the house like a military camp. She keeps everything spick and span. So whatever you do don't track any mud in on her freshly mopped floors."

"Matthew Colton is another person you'll meet in there. He's Jed's best friend. They've known each other since they were both knee-high to a June bug. He runs the freight company, but spends most of his time goin' on adventures with Jed and Hargy."

"Hargy?" Velvet tilted her head.

"Professor Phineas B. Hargroves." Pat chuckled. "He's got more brains than sense and once built a steam-powered pressure cooker that set half the kitchen on fire."

Pat paused for a moment and looked sheepishly down at the little cat.

"Although, I might've had a little to do with that when I cranked the pressure higher than he recommended."

Velvet's eyes widened a little and ears turned back slightly as he said that last part.

Pat suddenly cleared his throat. "Right. So, uh… I've been thinkin'. Might be best if we don't roll up with you lookin' like you're headin' to a cat masquerade."

Velvet's eyes shifted toward him.

"I mean no offense," Pat said quickly, hands raised. "It's just… folks here ain't used to cats wearin' vests, top hats and goggles. Might cause a bit of a stir, what with all the preparations being made for the important visitor coming here in a couple of days."

"You want me to hide, don't you?" Velvet said, her ears flattening in offense.

"Just till we get settled," Pat offered gently. "Panther, Dottie—why don't y'all hop in the crate? Just for show. And Velvet, if you don't mind crawlin' under the tarp next to it, you can pop out once we get around back and people ain't starin'."

Dottie hopped down immediately. "I don't mind. Crate's lined with straw."

Panther hesitated. "We better get treats for this."

"I got some canned tuna back at the house. I'll give each of you some if you just play along!" Pat promised the three felines.

With a reluctant sigh, Velvet stood, adjusted her hat with her paw, and gave a regal flick of her tail. "Fine. But I expect a proper introduction, later. No 'just some cat I found on the road' nonsense."

"Wouldn't dream of it," Pat grinned.

As Dottie and Panther slipped into the open-topped crate in the back of the wagon, settling among the straw, Velvet gave one last glance at the ranch on the horizon, then ducked beneath the canvas tarp with a faint hmph.

Pat adjusted his hat, gave the reins a little snap, and the wagon rolled on toward the gate.

As they finally reached the stately Victorian manor, Velvet peeked from under the edge of the canvas tarp. Her eyes widened.

Several men from the Davenport Freight Company were hauling ornate chairs, cabinets, and settees toward the front porch. Others were toting simpler furnishings into the nearby barn.

Velvet hissed at the men and ducked back under the tarp.

"Welcome to the new and improved Davenport Ranch," Pat said under his breath with a chuckle, hopping down from the wagon. "Now stay put Velvet, I'll get your adopted brother and sister inside, then come back for you."

He grabbed the crate holding Panther and Dottie with both hands and waddled around the side of the house toward the kitchen door, boots thudding against the wooden steps.

Velvet slipped out from beneath the tarp, leaped lightly onto the ground, and hid under the wagon. Her tail flicked. "What sort of ranch has a piano like that?"

Pat returned a moment later, sweat dotting his brow. "Okay, now you." He pulled the tarp back but didn't see the little black cat anywhere. "Velvet! Where are you?"

Suddenly, the little cat darted out from under the wagon and jumped gracefully into his arms. He tossed an apron over her and laughed, thinking how she felt like a squirming sack of flour.

"Just gotta stay hid a little longer while I go change into whatever ridiculous outfit the Professor picked out for me and Aggie to wear."

Inside, the house was a whirlwind—someone was yelling upstairs, a clatter echoed from the hall, and Agatha's voice rang out: "Pat! Where have you been?"

"Had to go pick up a couple of champion

mousers to take care of the issue in the barn." Pat motioned with his head toward the crate on the table. He kept his back to Agatha Porter, slipped into the pantry, and removed the apron. He gently set Velvet down and gave her a wink. "Stay low, stay quiet, and don't touch anything. I'll be back."

With that, he grabbed his new uniform hanging on the door, slung it over his shoulder, and raced down the hall.

Velvet sniffed the air and settled into a shadowy corner.

"This place is madness," she whispered. "Feels like home."

She sniffed the floor then suddenly dropped onto her side and stretched out before rolling over onto her back completely content.

****

For the next couple of hours, Velvet lay sleeping on the floor of the pantry as Pat Bennington and the others ran around in a frantic rush. Suddenly a long noise woke Velvet from her nap.

BANG!

The pantry door rattled as the sound of the kitchen door slamming open echoed through the room. Heavy boots stomped across the floor, followed by gasps and shrieks.

Velvet's eyes snapped open.

"What in the world—" Agatha Porter's voice cut off with a startled cry.

Velvet leaped to her feet and pressed herself low to the floor, her ears flattened.

The door to the pantry was cracked open just wide enough for her to peek out. That's when she spotted them!

She couldn't believe it. Not just one but two of Lady Seraphina Blackwood's guards were standing in the kitchen armed with atomic blaster rifles.

Velvet crouched lower. Her heart beat faster.

They'd found her again!

She spun in place, trying to stay quiet, her breathing shallow.

"*I have to get out of here!*" she frantically thought to herself.

Velvet retreated deep into the pantry, leaped over a stack of canned goods, and hid as best she could with her little top hat poking out from above the stack.

It was at this point she heard familiar footsteps and smelled a familiar scent. Lavender and woodsmoke. Lady Blackwood's voice echoed through the kitchen, ringing with authority. "Release whoever is in there and take up positions outside the door."

Velvet stayed motionless as the masked intruders filed out of the kitchen, their heavy boots

thudding against the floorboards before the outer
door slammed shut. She remained hidden for a
moment longer, her fur bristling and ears twitching.

Finally, she peeked out of the pantry. There
wasn't a single human in the room. Both Pat
Bennington and Agatha Porter were gone. Then she
heard voices from the hallway—familiar ones.

"...Who's this, Jed? Another one of those
troublemakers?" Pat's voice.

Velvet pushed the pantry door open further with
a gentle nudge of her paw, just enough to slip out.
Her movements were stealthy and silent. She
stayed low, keeping to the shadows.

Agatha's voice rang out next, sharp and
indignant. "You mind explaining why your goons
barged in on us like that? I just knew any minute
we were going to end up thrown in the corner,
stacked up like cordwood!"

Velvet's whiskers twitched. She peered around
the edge of the counter just in time to see Pat and
Agatha standing near the hallway entrance. That's
when she saw her! Lady Seraphina Blackwood
stood tall in the corridor beyond, her expression
calm and poised despite the tension in the room.

When Seraphina coolly insisted that Pat and
Agatha return to the kitchen, Velvet seized the
opportunity.

The little black cat darted into the hallway,
hugging the floor as she slipped past the pair, who

were too preoccupied to notice.

Voices echoed as Lady Seraphina, Jedidiah Davenport, and Matthew Colton entered the front room.

Velvet spotted an open door on the left—a small coat closet. Without hesitation, she slipped into the shadows and curled herself low among the boots and winter cloaks, her ears perked and alert.

From her hiding spot, she could clearly hear the conversation unfolding in the parlor.

Lady Blackwood was speaking, her voice steady and refined.

"She's here for me," Velvet's fur prickled. "I don't know how but she's found me."

But instead of mentioning the little black cat, Lady Seraphina began saying something about a relic. The Order of the Clockwork Octopus. Time and space. As the conversation continued, Velvet's heart slowly began to steady. Seraphina never mentioned her. Never uttered her name. Never gave a single command to search the premises.

Velvet narrowed her eyes and leaned in closer. "She's not here for me... She doesn't even know I'm here." That's when she suddenly began to recognize what the aristocratic human was talking about. It was the thing in the drawing she had seen so many times back on Seraphina's airship. The chronomechanism.

Velvet was just starting to ease back out of the

closet when a sudden crash echoed from above—
followed by a flailing, tumbling whump-whump-
whump of someone barreling down the staircase.

Velvet froze.

It was at this moment that Phineas B. Hargroves
landed in a heap at the bottom of the stairs.

What followed was chaos: shouts, questions, a
dramatic warning about an airship, and Phineas'
immediate realization that Lady Seraphina was in
the room. Velvet watched through the slit in the
door as he tried to recover his dignity and failed
spectacularly.

And then, Lady Seraphina turned and made for
the exit.

Velvet pressed her face closer to the doorframe,
eyes locked on the woman's flowing cloak and the
two masked guards who appeared in her path. She
remained still, barely breathing.

The front door opened. The porch creaked.
Outside, the faint thrum of the Aetherwind stirred
the evening air.

As everyone walked outside, Velvet made a run
for it. She dashed out of the closet, hopped up on
the window sill, and peered through the glass from
behind the curtains. She caught a glimpse of the
sleek airship, Lady Seraphina standing tall next to
the railing. Her guards silent at her side.

The ship rose with eerie grace, its engines
humming as it ascended into the darkening sky.

Velvet stared after it, green eyes narrowed.

"She's gone…" she whispered, barely audible. Her tail gave a relieved flick. "But she didn't come all this way for nothing..."

With the last rays of the setting sun catching the glinting off of the departing vessel, the Aetherwind disappeared into the clouds.

But even as the sky grew quiet, Velvet couldn't shake the feeling that Seraphina's visit had stirred something far more dangerous than anyone realized.

CHAPTER IV

The Night of a Thousand Rats

Almost afraid to move, Velvet continued staring outside, her tail flicking slowly. She had to make sure Seraphina really wasn't coming back.

"She's really gone," she finally let out a meow of relief. And with that, she finally slipped down from the windowsill and padded back across the hall.

Just as she did, the front door opened and footsteps thudded inside. It was the humans, Jedidiah Davenport, Matthew Colton, and Phineas B. Hargroves returning. Velvet darted back into the kitchen before they could see her.

She ran straight to Pat Bennington to let him know about the trouble she smelled in the air.

"What is it, girl?" The rotund man bent over and picked up the little black cat before his coworker could see it and placed her in the crate with Dottie and Panther. "You don't like that snooty woman either, do you?"

"Hold that thought!" Before Velvet could reply, Pat closed the lid and waddled away. "I just remembered I forgot to do something!"

"What did you forget?" Agatha Porter called after the comical older man.

"To listen in on their conversation in the other room!" He chuckled.

"Dottie, Panther—wake up." Velvet nudged her adopted siblings with her nose.

Panther cracked one eye open. "Dinner?"

"No," she said, slowly. "Something's wrong."

Before she could explain she felt a sudden jarring motion as the crate was being lifted off the table. Agatha Porter had had enough of cats being in the house and decided to put them outside on the service porch.

It was around this time that Pat Bennington came back into the room. "Got caught snooping quicker than I thought!" He laughed and then spotted Agatha carrying the cats outside.

"Now hold on, Aggy!" The rotund man waddled over and took the crate from her. "I was just about to take them out back to take care of that little job they were hired to do!"

The older woman stepped back as he pushed past her and started towards the barn. A few minutes later, Pat set the crate down with a grunt, brushing off his hands.

"Alright, kids this is your new home and your new place of employment. They say it's been completely overrun by furry little varmints. But I'm sure you can take care of that problem."

But before any cat could move, Panther poked his head out and let out a low, impressed meow.

The barn wasn't empty. Not even close.

Nestled between bales of hay and stacks of feed sacks were several pieces of mismatched furniture. Jedidiah Davenport's old parlor set, now clearly demoted to barn duty. There were velvet-upholstered settees, a brocade armchair with a sun-faded cushion, and even a carved wooden footstool with lion's-paw legs.

"Ohhhh," Dottie purred, peering over the edge of the crate. "They put all this out here just for us?"

Velvet narrowed her eyes in appreciation. "Pat you must've gone to a lot of trouble to make sure we're comfortable out here."

"Well actually..." Pat started to tell them the truth about the furniture but decided not to. "Nothing's too good for champion mousers like the three of you." He chuckled to himself as he turned back toward the barn doors. "It's a good thing you are all house-trained. This furniture wouldn't last a week otherwise."

"I've got to go back to the house and take care of my chores. You three make me proud and take care of our little rodent problem."

And with that, he waddled off, leaving the barn door just slightly ajar.

The second he was gone, all three cats leaped from the crate in synchronized silence like a team of trained acrobats.

Velvet landed with a soft thump on the seat of a high-backed armchair and immediately rolled onto her side, stretching out luxuriously. "Finally. A chair worthy of my presence."

Panther belly-flopped onto the fainting couch with a happy sigh. "I could nap here for days."

Dottie hopped daintily onto the ottoman, kneaded it twice, then flopped over in delight. "It's like lounging on a marshmallow wrapped in royalty."

The barn echoed briefly with soft purrs of satisfaction.

Then—instinct kicked in.

Velvet stood, turned toward the armrest, and extended her claws with a satisfying *shkkt*. She gave the material a slow, deliberate rake.

Panther followed suit, digging into the settee with both front paws. "Just helping break it in."

Dottie joined in, working the side of the ottoman like it owed her money.

Velvet paused just long enough to sigh contentedly.

"Barn life isn't so bad," she murmured.

That's when the first creak came from the

shadows.

Velvet heard it but didn't move.

Her ears twitched.

Somewhere deep inside the barn... something was moving. Something she couldn't quite make out by scent.

Panther yawned, stretched, and looked around. "What do you smell? Pat back with the tuna?"

"Quiet!" Velvet hissed as she dropped to the floor.

Panther and Dottie immediately sensed the same danger as Velvet and became on guard.

For a few moments, the barn was still.

Velvet padded forward, ears twitching. "Something doesn't feel right."

Panther dropped to the ground and sniffed at a pile of grain. "I don't smell anything."

"That's because your sniffer is too young." Dottie hissed as she hopped up onto a feed barrel to get a better look around. "It's not matured like mine and Velvet's"

Dottie hopped back down and trotted over next to the slightly older cat. "What is it we smell?" She asked.

Velvet hissed for her to be quiet too. "We're not alone in here!"

Panther groaned. "Can't we just take a nap and let whatever's in here wake us up when they're ready to play?" He laid down on a nearby pile of hay and curled up into a ball.

"Panther," Velvet said without turning, "if you don't get your lazy tail up right now, I'll tell Pat you only like to be fed twice a day instead of your normal six to eight feedings."

Panther gasped. "You wouldn't!"

Velvet gave him a flat look. "Try me."

"Okay, okay..."

The three cats split off, slipping into the deeper corners of the barn as shadows lengthened across the floor. Somewhere inside the large structure, something creaked.

Panther froze. "Did you hear that?"

Velvet paused. "Yes."

Dottie's ears twitched. "I think it was just the wind."

Velvet narrowed her eyes, her voice dropping low. "Let's stay sharp."

Just then, a loud clang echoed from across the barn.

All three cats froze.

Panther whispered, "That wasn't the wind."

A second sound followed—scraping, like claws across the wood. Then another bang.

Panther started making low growling noises as he stepped behind Dottie.

A scrabble of claws echoed from the far corner, and a shape lunged from the shadows.

"Showtime!" Dottie screamed as she launched

herself at the oncoming figure.

It was huge. A rat every bit as big as she was came barreling into the light with yellow eyes and teeth like piano keys. Dottie collided with the rat mid-leap, the two of them slamming into the settee. A loud *rrrriiiip* sounded as claws tore through fabric and stuffing exploded like snowflakes into the air.

"Dottie!" Velvet shouted, springing forward.

But before either she or Panther could reach her, something unexpected happened.

With a final hiss and a kick from Dottie's hind legs, the rat staggered back... and its entire fur coat slipped off in one perfect piece.

There was a screech of metal and a spark.

Velvet and Panther froze.

At first, Dottie didn't realize what was going on until she looked down and realized she was holding a fake fur coat in her teeth. She looked over at the rat she had been scuffling with and her mouth fell open as she dropped the fur to the ground.

Suddenly, from among the bales of hay and storage crates, more pairs of glowing red eyes began to appear.

"Run!" Velvet shouted.

The three cats scrambled toward the barn door, slipped past it, and ran into the night, tails low, ears perked. Once they were a safe distance away, they turned and reassessed the situation.

A wall-mounted lantern flickered inside the barn, left lit by one of the workers. The door was still open enough for Velvet to spot movement inside.

Low. Fast. Skittering.

The sounds echoing from inside weren't organic but mechanical.

Panther whispered, "That's not a normal rat."

"No," Velvet said. Her voice dropped to a growl. "Its something else."

Velvet crouched low. "Do you see what I see?"

The rat that Dottie had pulled the fur coat off of stepped into view. It wasn't what any of them had previously expected. It had a completely metal body with a tail that clanked as it dragged against the floor. Steam hissed softly from vents along its spine.

Panther swore under his breath. "You didn't say we were fighting zombie rats."

"They're not zombie rats," Dottie said shakily. "They're..."

"Rattomatons!" Velvet bared her teeth.

"What's that?" Dottie asked, wide-eyed, her ears laid back.

"They're not real," Velvet explained. "They're made of brass, and copper, and filled with springs and cogs! I've seen photographs of them."

"Robo mice?" Panther chimed in.

"Yes!"

"How did they get in the barn?" Dottie growled at the mere thought of their new home being invaded.

"I don't know," Velvet hissed. "But, they're about to find out it was the worst mistake they've ever made!"

"We can't take on rat... ratta... rat... a..." Panther struggled to pronounce the word and finally gave up. "We can't bite through brass and copper!"

Even Dottie admitted it was a fight she didn't think they could win.

"Not with that attitude we can't!" Velvet's ears laid back and she arched her back as she marched in front of Dottie and Panther. "Are the two of you forgetting your heritage?"

The two little black cats looked at each confused.

"We're not just cats. We come from a long line of strong felines!" Velvet stopped pacing and sat still as she wrapped her tail around her feet. She tilted her head and looked off in thought. "Take Princess Bonita for example!"

"Who?" Panther trilled. He had never heard this story before but was anxious to hear more.

"Princess Bonita!" Velvet hissed. "Maybe you know her by her common name, Fuzzy Face? I was actually named after her. My name is Velvet Face."

Panther showed no reaction so Velvet continued her story.

"Princess Bonita, also known to her enemies as Fuzzy the Ferocious, was heir to the throne of Catopia. She was kidnapped at a very young age and taken away to a strange land by an Opossum and a Racoon. But do you think she gave up?"

Velvet's troop was beginning to get encouraged. "No!" They meowed in unison.

"And what about the legend of Saber?" She asked them. "When five dogs came around threatening the safety of her newborn kittens did she run?"

"Maybe..." Panther began sheepishly.

"No!" Dottie meowed.

"...No!" Panther quickly changed his answer.

"That's right!" Velvet began to trill excitedly. "She made all five of those dogs tuck their tails between their legs and run for the hills! A common little cat!"

Dottie's fur puffed up. Panther stood taller than he had all evening.

With a new spark in their eyes, both turned and stood shoulder to shoulder with their newly adopted sister.

Velvet narrowed her gaze at the barn.

"Time to show those scrap piles what real cats are made of."

With a flick of their tails, they leaped!

Charging into the barn together, paws pounding against the floorboards, tails slicing through the air like pennants in battle. Even Dottie's little bobbed tail stood proud as they stormed in.

The moment they reentered, the Rattomatons turned.

There were more of them now.

Six in total to be specific.

Their eyes, glowing red now, narrowed in unison. Tiny clawed feet scraped the floor. One emitted a high-pitched mechanical squeal that echoed like a kettle reaching a boil.

"We can handle this. There's just two a piece for us," Velvet noted. "Split up and keep them off balance!"

Panther dove left behind a sack of feed. Dottie veered right, already howling her war cry.

The Rattomatons lunged.

Dottie met one mid-air again, this time flipping it over with a precision kick. It crashed into a storage barrel, but a second caught her from behind and sent her sprawling.

Panther scampered up a post and ran along a beam overhead. "I'll drop from above!" he shouted —just as one of the Rattomatons skittered up the post behind him.

"Oh no! This one has grappling legs!" he cried. "IT'S CLIMBING LIKE A SPIDER!"

Velvet launched herself at two closing in on the grain sacks, drawing their attention. She slashed at a thin pipe on one's back that was sticking out from under its fake fur. Steam hissed out, and the Rattomaton whirled in confusion before crashing sideways.

Meanwhile, Dottie rolled across the floor with a clattering enemy tangled in her claws. "Not so tough without your fur coat, are ya?!" She bit into the metal housing and immediately yelped in pain. "Maybe you're a little bit tough!"

Panther, cornered on the beam, made a split-second decision and jumped.

He landed on the largest rattomaton with an undignified WHUMP, sending it sliding into the wall. Panther used the momentum to leap sideways and launch himself onto the armchair. The cushion gave a pitiful wheeze as tufts of stuffing puffed out of a long tear, as he slid down it.

"Dottie!" he called out panicked. "Help!"

"I'm kind of busy!" She replied as she continued rolling around on the floor wrestling with her metal rodent.

"Just ride it like the humans ride the horses!" Velvet trilled.

"I think it's taking me for a ride!"

"Try to steer it into a wall!" Dottie suggested as she grabbed her Rattomaton by its mechanical tail and slung it into a pail of water.

"How? I don't have reins or a saddle!"

Still, he clung to its head and bit down on a loose wire. Sparks flew. The Rattomaton juddered, then collapsed beneath him in a heap of twisted brass.

Panther stood and raised one paw. "Victory!"

His celebration was short-lived as he was plowed into the side and knocked over by another charging metal rat.

Dottie spotted the one still up in the rafters and climbed up after it. She rammed it full speed and sent it flying. They both began a free fall to the hard ground below. Dottie however flipped around in mid-air and managed to land on all four paws completely unharmed. The Rattomaton however, rattled to the ground in a clang of defeat.

As soon as she had her bearings she raced over to Panther and helped him with the mechanical rodent he was battling. The two of them together quickly subdued it. This left one remaining Rattomaton. All three cats made short order of him in no time flat.

Panting heavily, Velvet scanned the room. Still catching her breath from their hard-fought victory.

The barn was quiet again.

The wreckage of all six Rattomatons now lay scattered across the barn and Jedidiah's furniture also had a few battle scars.

"We did it," Dottie meowed. "We actually did it."

Panther groaned as he walked over and curled up under a wheelbarrow. "Don't wake me up until next week or until breakfast is served."

"Wait," Velvet said, her tail flicking. "I don't think this is over."

From the back of the barn, a creaking sound rose.

Wood shifted.

Something moved.

Then—eyes.

More glowing red dots blinked to life in the darkness. Not six. Not ten. More like dozens. They started coming from everywhere. Some clung to rafters like iron spiders, lining the beams. Others were crawling out from under crates. The ones above began lowering themselves like marionettes.

Panther perked up from his resting spot and gulped. "Didn't they get the telegram? The battle is over. We won!"

"No," Velvet crouched low, her claws unsheathing with a soft *shkkt*. "They were just warming up, but so were we!"

"This is going to be a long night, isn't it?" Panther winced as he uncurled his body and stood to his paws.

"I've got no plans!" Dottie growled, crouching low beside Velvet as she prepared for the next wave.

"Remember what Saber did to those five dogs?" Velvet hissed. "Let's multiply that by twenty."

Panther fell in line on her other side, fur puffed

Velvet stood in the middle, ready to fight. Dottie growled and crouched low beside her, while Panther fell in line on her other side.

like a feather duster.

"Time to find out if they run on steam or fear!" Velvet trilled as she led the charge.

Throughout the rest of the night, they battled hard against the mechanical rats until finally, the three feline siblings had won the battle. There wasn't a single mechanical rodent left standing. Velvet picked up her top hat and goggles with her teeth and curled up beside her adopted siblings inside the open crate.

Bruised, tired, and victorious, she said, "Next time, we're charging per rat!"

"What about our new furniture?" Dottie meowed sleepily as she looked around at the mess everything was in.

"Just looks lived in, to me..." Panther yawned before drifting off to sleep.

CHAPTER V

A Cat Among Gears

Early the next morning, sunbeams began to spill through the hay loft, warming Velvet's fur where she lay curled in the straw-lined crate beside Panther and Dottie. Around them, the barn was quiet—save for the faint creaks of wooden beams and the occasional sleepy snore from Panther.

Brass fragments, twisted springs, and dented gears lay strewn across the floor like the aftermath of a mechanical storm. Bits of fur-covered casings, snapped tails, and dozens of shattered glass lenses glinted in the morning light. Not to mention all the shredded furniture.

The barn door creaked open further.

"Land o' Goshen!" Pat Bennington's voice broke the silence like a bell. "What in the name of burnt biscuits happened in here?"

Velvet stirred faintly.

His boots thudded softly across the barn floor as

he surveyed the battlefield—dozens of defeated rattomatons in various states of disassembly, their inner workings laid bare.

"I leave y'all alone one night," he muttered, picking up a cog and flicking it aside, "and you turn the place into a scrapyard."

"Oh dear, oh dear..." He stepped carefully around the wreckage, lifting a snapped mechanical tail with a wince before letting it clatter back to the floor. "Good thing Jed's about to take off with the others," he added under his breath. "If he saw this, he'd think the barn got invaded by a whole clockwork circus."

Velvet's eyes blinked open at the sound of Pat's voice. She yawned, stretched once, and peered out from the crate.

Pat noticed her movement and worriedly asked. "Velvet? What in tarnation happened?"

She sat up slowly, yawned, and started rubbing a paw across one ear. Her hat and goggles were still lying neatly beside her, just where she'd left them. She tilted her head and gave Pat a curious look.

"Did the three of you get into the Professor's box of spare parts?" He took a few more steps, picking up a bit of singed wiring and shaking his head. "At least I'll have time to clean everything up while Jed and the others are in St. Louis running an errand for that Blackwood lady."

Velvet froze. Her ears shot up.

"Lady Seraphina Blackwood?" she meowed, suddenly wide awake. "He's going on a mission for her?"

Pat raised an eyebrow. "Yeah. He just finished breakfast and is getting ready to leave. Why?"

Velvet sprang to her feet. "Put my hat on."

Pat blinked. "Your hat? Why?"

She grabbed the top hat with her teeth and leaped over the side of the crate. "Put my hat and goggles on, now!"

"Okay..." The rotund man took the hat from her and placed it on his own head. "It's not a perfect fit but now what?"

"On me!" She snapped. "Put it and my goggles on me and hurry. I have to be on that airship when it takes off!"

Pat stared at her for a second, then gave a low whistle. "Well, that does make more sense but why do you need to be aboard the Swift?"

Velvet stood tall, tail flicking with purpose. "I can't explain it now but I have to go with them!"

He bent down, carefully settling the little top hat on her head, then slipped the brass goggles over the brim and adjusted her ears through the holes. "You sure about this?" he asked softly, crouching beside her. "It could be dangerous."

She looked up at him, green eyes steady. "Danger is my middle name."

"I thought it was Face." Panther raised his furry

head up and blinked his eyes. "Or is Face your last name? Velvet Danger Face..."

"Not now!" She hissed at him.

"Just wake me when there's tuna," Panther laid his head back down and flipped over on his other side.

Pat gave a single nod. "Alright. Then let's get you aboard that airship."

Velvet gave a firm meow of thanks—and together, she and Pat Bennington made for the distant hangar.

The little black cat and the rotund man climbed into a nearby wagon and started down the path that wound beyond the main house and into a valley. The morning sun flickered over the dew-covered grass.

Velvet hopped down from the wagon as they approached the hangar. She crouched low and stealthily made her way toward the ship while Pat distracted Jed and the others with sandwiches he had prepared for their trip.

Jedidiah Davenport stood with Jonathan Blake and Matthew Colton near the airship's loading ramp, reviewing a chart one last time. Velvet spotted them through the wide entry and pressed herself low to the ground.

As they were thanking him for their lunch basket, Velvet made her way up the ramp completely undetected. She immediately slipped behind some crates in the cargo hold.

Suddenly, with a rising hum, the engines roared to life.

The airship was taking off with Steampunk Velvet as its official stowaway.

****

Four hours later, the crew of the Swift arrived in St. Louis, Missouri. It was now 2PM on October 21, 1881.

The sudden descent jarred Velvet from her nap behind a few crates.

She stretched, blinking at the light filtering through the cracks in the hold.

Velvet crept forward, her goggles bouncing lightly as she padded toward a small porthole. She rose onto her hind legs and peered through the glass.

Below, brick buildings lined a narrow street. The Mississippi glittered in the distance beneath the afternoon sun. Chimneys belched lazy columns of smoke into the sky, and a maze of warehouse rooftops stretched in every direction.

The airship had touched down in a secluded clearing tucked behind a grove of trees, well out of sight from the main road. A perfect hiding spot.

The humming engines quieted to a purr, then faded entirely. Outside, muffled voices drifted through the cargo bay's walls—Jedidiah, Jonathan, and Matthew preparing to disembark.

Velvet darted back into the shadows, crouching behind a coil of rope just as footsteps passed overhead. Through a gap in the floorboards, she watched as boots thudded down the gangplank. Jedidiah led the way, followed by Jonathan and Matthew.

As they disappeared into the trees, Velvet waited—counting slowly in her head.

One... two... three...

When the grove finally swallowed the last sound of their boots, she climbed out of the cargo hold and descended the loading ramp. The tall grass brushed her fur as she slipped from shadow to shadow, ears twitching at every chirp and creak.

The scent of oil, rust, and old machinery grew stronger as she neared the cluster of warehouses. Velvet pressed herself against the cold brick wall of the nearest building and glanced around the corner.

The three men were already slipping through a narrow alleyway.

Velvet followed.

Careful not to let her brass goggles glint in the light, she stayed a full building length behind, zigzagging from barrel to crate, from window ledge to ledge.

Finally, she watched them disappear through an unmarked door in the side of a warehouse.

The metal door hissed shut.

Velvet stared for a long moment, then padded closer, ears perked. A vent near the ground—just wide enough. She sniffed it. Dust. Oil. Metal. No recent food scents. Perfect.

She wriggled inside.

The duct carried the echo of voices ahead. Velvet crawled slowly, following the vibrations and light until a faint golden glow began to dance on the walls.

She stopped at a grated opening. Below, the vast, gleaming expanse of the Clockwork Conqueror's hidden workshop unfolded.

Velvet's eyes widened.

Every surface was covered in inventions. Spindly machines, towering suits of armor, half-finished automatons suspended on chains—parts of them twitching like they were dreaming. On a far table, glowing tubes bubbled faintly, and glass spheres hummed with pent-up energy.

Velvet's nose wrinkled at the smell of scorched copper and aged grease.

She was just about to inch forward when she froze.

A faint clink echoed from somewhere in the ductwork—a sound too sharp, too intentional. Not the hum of machines or the groan of old metal, but something moving. Something alive.

She backed away from the grate and crawled

toward the noise, ears pinned flat. The duct narrowed, curved, and finally opened into a small chamber—a hollow crawlspace nestled behind a wall of riveted steel.

A figure stood inside, partially cloaked in shadow.

Velvet crouched low and narrowed her eyes. She recognized the brass mask first—ornate and polished, its lenses glinting in the gloom.

"Why does this human look so familiar?" She meowed gently to herself. Then suddenly it dawned on her. It was the Clockwork Conqueror!

She still remembered very clearly the day Seraphina Blackwood threw that letter opener across the room impaling the photo of him on the wall.

The Conqueror didn't move a muscle, his mechanical hand resting on the wall in front of him. A small peephole was cut into the metal, and he was peering through it—watching the workshop floor.

Velvet's fur bristled. Her tail flicked once. Whatever he was planning, she couldn't let it play out.

Silently, she turned and scrambled back the way she came, paws barely making a sound. She reached the grated opening and pressed her face against it, whiskers twitching as she searched for a gap.

It looked solid—too narrow to squeeze through —but as she gave it a tentative nudge with her shoulder, the entire panel creaked... then swung open with a soft groan.

Velvet blinked in surprise as she slipped through without hesitation, landing with a light thud on a nearby shelf cluttered with gears.

Then, without warning, she leaped to the floor and darted across the path of the three humans. Velvet stopped and stared directly at them, her piercing green eyes catching the golden light of the overhead chandelier.

For a moment, none of them moved. Jonathan Blake squinted, his mouth opening slightly before snapping shut. Jedidiah Davenport tilted his head, his brow furrowed, as though trying to make sense of what he was seeing. Matthew Colton's grip on his lantern tightened, his knuckles whitening as he unconsciously shifted back a step.

Suddenly, Velvet turned and darted down the corridor, disappearing into the shadows.

Instinctively, she knew the three men would follow. Velvet raced down the metal hall as fast as her four paws could carry her.

She skidded to a halt at the end of the corridor where the heavy metal door loomed—sealed tight just as she'd feared. Her ears flicked at the faint sounds of pursuit behind her. No time to panic.

A small wall panel sat just above her head, its

Velvet leading the way
back through the corridor.

levers and toggles dusty with disuse. Velvet narrowed her eyes. This was something she was familiar with. Lady Serphina had one on each side of the door to her private cabin aboard her airship.

It wasn't identical, but it was close enough.

Velvet sprang upward, her front paws slapping at the lowest lever. It didn't budge. Bracing one rear foot on a pipe, she launched again—this time dragging the switch down with a sharp, determined swipe.

With a clunk and a hiss, something shifted behind the wall. A second lever began to twitch on its own, rising slowly.

The door at the end of the hallway creaked open with a faint, echoing groan.

Velvet immediately hopped down and ran through it. She ducked into the tall grass just beyond the threshold, crouching low as the men's footsteps drew closer, muttering about the door being open when they knew they'd closed it. She waited, tense, watching the shadows stretch across the doorway. One by one, the three men emerged into the sunlight.

Satisfied they were safe, Velvet turned and bolted, weaving through the brush and looping around wide—always staying ahead, but keeping the three men in sight.

By the time the human trio reached the Swift, she was already inside, hidden once more behind a stack of crates in the cargo hold, her hat, vest, and goggles miraculously all still in place while her tail flicked with nervous energy.

As the men climbed aboard and the airship lifted off, Matthew leaned against the railing, his brow furrowed. "Okay, I have to ask," he said, breaking the silence. "That cat... Did it look... odd to either of you?"

Velvet's keen ears twitched as she heard that question. "Odd? You should see how you humans look to us cats!" She hissed.

The engines began to hum again, rising to a steady thrum as the Swift lifted into the sky.

She crouched lower, ears perked as the conversation became harder to hear.

In her mind, Velvet could picture them standing by the railing, trying to make sense of what they'd seen. The tone of Matthew's voice said everything —half unsure, half certain he'd just witnessed something his brain couldn't quite explain.

A long pause. Then nervous laughter. Then more silence.

Velvet smirked.

"They act like they've never seen a cat wearing a vest, top hat, and goggles before."

CHAPTER VI

A Growl in the Dark

For the next hour and a half, the Swift soared quietly through the Missouri sky, its polished brass trim catching the fading light of dusk. Inside the cargo hold, Velvet lay nestled atop a folded canvas tarp beside a coil of rope. Her vest was still neatly in place. Her brass goggles rested atop her hat, and her green eyes gleamed with sleepy contentment.

"Humans," she murmured to herself with a purr. "They'd be helpless without me."

Above her, voices drifted faintly through the grates in the deck. Jedidiah Davenport was at the helm again, fiddling with the map they'd recovered. Matthew Colton stood nearby, clearly skeptical, and Jonathan Blake's voice carried with its usual calm logic as he cleaned his revolver.

Velvet yawned and stretched, her claws flexing gently against the tarp. "They never fail to overcomplicate things," she mused. "You want to know what's out there? Use your nose and find out!"

As the airship descended toward a densely wooded ridge, Velvet once again padded to a porthole, raised up on her back legs, and peered out. Below, the treetops shivered with the wind. A plume of smoke curled skyward near a rock formation.

"Woodsmoke," Velvet purred thoughtfully. "I can smell it from here."

By the time the Swift had been securely moored, Velvet had already slipped down the ramp's struts and vanished into the underbrush. She moved low, silent, shadow to shadow. The air was cooler down here, thick with pine and damp earth.

Up ahead, the humans moved carefully through the trees—Jedidiah in the lead, Jonathan close behind, Matthew trailing slightly but sharp-eyed as ever. However, he had no idea she was following them.

They came upon the cave just as the last rays of sun dipped behind the hills. Velvet kept her distance, watching from a rock outcropping above. The cave's mouth loomed like something alive, breathing slow, cold air into the forest.

As they lit their lanterns and disappeared inside, Velvet crouched and continued to follow from a safe distance.

The cave interior was a labyrinth.

The little black cat with a patch of white fur on her chest slinked along, climbing ledges and darting along stone ridges above the human path. Lantern light flickered on the walls, casting strange shadows across the ancient stone.

Whenever Matthew paused to look at the markings, Velvet studied them too. Her eyes narrowed. She didn't understand the words, but she sensed their importance.

Eventually, the three men entered a wide cavern lit only by their lanterns. Velvet perched on a rocky beam above, her tail flicking slowly. She stared at mounds of stolen loot strewn across the cave floor —bags of coins, silver, silks.

For a moment all was silent then a voice suddenly boomed from behind the three she had been trailing.

"Too bad you won't be getting out to tell anyone about it!"

Velvet dropped flat, ears back. She sniffed the air and smelled the scent of the newcomers. She was angry at herself for not realizing they were there sooner.

Boots scraped stone as four masked figures stepped into the lantern light, ray guns raised, green-glowing orbs humming with power. The leader's voice cut through the air like a blade.

"Don't even think about it."

Velvet's ears flattened even further as she bore

her teeth but didn't make a single noise. Jonathan Blake's hand hovered near his revolver. Matthew Colton looked ready to spring. Jedidiah Davenport stood firm, his expression hard.

Then—slowly—they obeyed.

Weapons hit the floor with dull thuds. The outlaws closed in. The leader, scarf covering his face, strutted forward, smug beneath the brim of his hat. "Turn around. Nice and slow."

One outlaw sneered. "Hey—I know you! You were on the train!"

The leader's eyes lit with fury as he stepped closer to Jedidiah. "You're the one who humiliated me."

Matthew stepped between them, hands raised. "He was trying to survive."

Words flew—accusations, questions about the Clockwork Conqueror, about the weapons. The outlaw scoffed. "We just buy what we're sold. Didn't ask who made 'em."

Velvet exhaled slowly, her claws flexing against the stone. The outlaw leader was furious and that made him dangerous. He held the upper hand.

Not for long though.

Velvet crept back along the beam, tail twitching. She found a narrow offshoot tunnel behind the wall and vanished into it. The passage was narrow, perfect for someone her size.

A few seconds later, from deep within the cave,

a low, echoing growl rumbled through the stone.

The outlaws snapped to attention. One turned. Another backed toward the wall.

Velvet crouched again and let out a second, louder growl—deep, guttural, and echoing off the cave walls made it sound nothing like a cat. It sounded like it belonged to something much larger. Something that didn't belong in a cave.

The panic she felt from them was instantaneous. Boots scraped stone once again. Fingers twitched nervously on their triggers.

"What was that?"

"Quiet!"

In that moment of hesitation, Jedidiah and Matthew saw their chance. They dropped to the ground, hands moving fast. Gunfire thundered through the cave. Glass shattered. Green liquid hissed and sparked.

Velvet crouched low, ears ringing, tail stiff.

When the smoke cleared, the outlaws stood frozen—locked mid-motion in eerie silence.

"Paralyzed," Jonathan whispered. "Completely paralyzed."

Velvet blinked. "You're welcome." But none of them heard her.

She watched as they gathered what they came for. For good measure, they even tossed the four ray guns into the burlap sacks they picked up from the pile.

Before they turned to leave, she crept forward from the shadows.

Velvet knew she couldn't wait around any longer or she might get left behind. Despite the fact that all three lanterns were raised, she stepped into the light.

They froze.

Velvet tilted her head, her goggles glinting. She let out a deep, low *mrrrrrow*, equal parts curiosity and warning.

Then, with theatrical poise only a cat could manage, she turned and vanished into the darkness.

****

Back aboard the Swift, soaring high beneath the moon, Velvet was once again curled up behind some cargo crates. She lay quietly, tail swishing, her top hat still resting on her head. Her green eyes blinked a few times as she yawned, stretched, curled up into a ball, and drifted off to sleep.

Later that night, the Swift touched down under the moonlit sky, its brass trim gleaming as the engines wound to a halt near the Victorian manor at Davenport Ranch. Inside, the aroma of stew and fresh bread filled the air.

All the humans sat around the kitchen table, lanterns glowing warmly as they sifted through sacks of recovered valuables. Silver gleamed.

Velvet crept forward from the shadows and
into the lantern light. Everyone froze.

Coins clinked. A familiar glint of brass caught Jedidiah's eye.

"There it is," he said, drawing out the pocket watch he'd set out to retrieve. Its green stone pulsed faintly as if it recognized its rightful owner.

Meanwhile, across the yard in the dim light of the barn, Velvet trotted through wet grass. Her vest was still neat, her hat slightly askew. She slipped in through a gap in the barn door and made a beeline for her adopted siblings.

"Velvet!" Dottie called, rushing out from a pile of straw. "You're back!"

Panther stretched and yawned. "You missed dinner and the rain storm."

Velvet shook the dust from her fur. "The two of you missed being shot at with alien weaponry. I'll trade you."

Before either of them could ask questions, the barn doors creaked open again.

Pat Bennington shuffled in, holding a chipped bowl brimming with tuna.

"There y'all are," he said, setting the bowl down in the straw. "Figured you might want a snack after all the chaos today."

The cats gathered around eagerly. Velvet took a bite, then narrowed her eyes as she looked around the barn.

The floor was swept, except for a few scraps of twisted brass, cracked lenses, and bits of mechanical debris that clung to a few bales of hay. All of the stuffing from the furniture had been shoved back in and the rotund man had done his best to sew the holes back up. However, they were still very visible.

Pat scratched his head. "Took me all afternoon to clean this place up. Still don't know what happened here. Looked like someone threw a tea party for a bunch of wind-up toys and forgot to invite me."

Velvet kept eating, hiding a smirk behind her whiskers.

Dottie looked at Panther. "Should we tell him?"

Panther snorted. "About the mechanical rats? Nah. Let him think it was a tea party."

Pat gave the cats a satisfied nod. "Anyway, y'all rest up. I got a feelin' tomorrow's gonna be another big day. Jed and the others are talking about going to Detroit to meet up with that high society lady again."

Velvet's ears perked up. She turned to ask Pat what he meant— but he was already gone.

The barn grew quiet again.

Velvet licked the last bit of tuna from her whiskers, curled up between Dottie and Panther, and let out a low, contented purr.

"Try not to snore too much tonight," she murmured.

"We missed you too," Dottie yawned.

And with that, the barn settled into silence—save for the gentle clink of wind chimes outside and three well-fed cats drifting off to sleep.

Velvet still wasn't entirely sure what she'd gotten herself into, but she knew exactly where she was going next.

"Detroit," she murmured, curling tighter. "I'm going to Detroit."

****

Early the next morning, sunlight once again spilled in dusty streaks through the slats of the barn wall, warming the straw in patches. Velvet blinked awake, ears twitching at the sound of human voices outside—boots crunching gravel, harnesses jingling, and the low, excited murmur of final preparations.

She stretched luxuriously, her claws kneading the straw beneath her. Her top hat had tumbled off in the night and lay crookedly beside her.

The barn door creaked open.

"Morning, kitties," Pat Bennington called in his usual gravelly drawl as he stepped in, balancing a dented metal tray. "Brought ya some leftovers from yesterday."

Velvet's nose twitched. She sat up quickly.

"Stew?" she guessed.

"Yup," Pat said proudly, setting the bowl down.

"Figured y'all deserved a warm breakfast."

Panther was already padding over, tail high. Dottie bounced behind him, eyes wide.

But Velvet stayed put.

"What's all the noise outside?" she asked, swishing her tail back and forth.

"Oh, that's just Jed and the others preparing to leave."

"Hat!" Velvet meowed aggressively.

The rotund man chuckled as he reached down to pick it up. "Here we go again!"

"Hurry!" She growled. "I have to be on the Swift before they take off without me."

Pat blinked at her, then let out a low chuckle.

"Swift?" he shook his head. "Hate to break it to ya, but they ain't takin' the Swift this time. It's the Phoenix they're loadin' up."

Velvet's ears perked. "The Phoenix? What's that?"

"It's one of Jed's other airships," Pat explained as he helped the little cat to get into her outfit. "It's been outta commission for a few weeks thanks to some low-down varmint that sabotaged it. Jed nearly ripped the whole bottom out when they crash-landed just outside of Spoon Fork. But the professor's been fixin' it up ever since. Says it's even better than it was before. Better, stronger, faster."

Velvet's tail flicked anxiously. "Then which way

do I go?"

Pat scratched behind his ear. "Determined, ain't ya?" The bearded man waddled to the door and pointed in the general direction of the hangar.

Velvet raced over beside him, top hat now neatly secured between her ears.

"Well," she said, voice full of quiet determination, "then I suppose I'd better get moving!"

Pat grinned as she strutted past him.

"Be careful. Just don't get too hungry. It's gonna be a long flight."

"I hadn't thought about that..." Without another word, Velvet turned and rushed back into the barn. With her teeth, she grabbed the handle of the bowl and took off with the stew.

"Hey!" Dottie and Panther hissed.

"Don't worry, kids," Pat laughed, turning back toward the house. "Plenty more leftover stew where that came from!"

Meanwhile, Velvet continued on her path toward the newly repaired airship, tail high, paws silent on the path.

Finally, not one but two hangars loomed ahead. Pat hadn't told her there were twin buildings here. However, it wasn't hard for her to figure out which one housed the Phoenix. It was the one with all the humans going in and out of it.

Stealthily she crouched low to the ground and

snuck inside using a side door. That's when she spotted it. Its hull a polished patchwork of brass, rivets, and polished wood. The building's open roof allowed the morning sunlight to dance off its freshly burnished trim, glinting like armor ready for battle. Steam hissed softly from inside the vessel as the crew loaded the last of the supplies.

Velvet crouched low behind a crate, the stolen stew bowl gripped firmly in her teeth. Her eyes scanned the path to the airship's open cargo ramp.

"Too exposed," she muttered through her bite, tail twitching.

Nearby, Jedidiah's voice rang out as he checked the engine readouts with Matthew. Phineas wandered into a workshop attached to the building, oblivious.

Velvet darted forward—silent, a black streak of fur and determination. She slid behind a wagon wheel leaned against the wall, then under a canvas tarp, then behind a stack of shipping crates marked Davenport Dispatch & Delivery Company.

A dropped wrench clattered nearby, but no one looked her way.

"Perfect."

She slinked along the shadows until she reached the base of the loading ramp. Still balancing the stew bowl in her mouth, she lowered her head and barreled ahead. She wasted no time in making her way into the cargo hold. She weaved between stacked crates and tucked herself neatly into a corner.

Just in time.

Footsteps echoed as Matthew Colton strolled over to where she was. He dropped a satchel by the wall and called to the upper deck, "We're good down here, Jed!"

Velvet froze, breathing slowly. He passed within a whisker's breadth of her hiding spot.

"Too close," she meowed to herself. She wriggled further behind the crates until she found a narrow crawlspace between two support beams. A ragged wool blanket had been tossed there, along with a discarded map tube large enough to fit her. After setting the stew down, she used her teeth to pull the blanket partway into the tube. After that she curled inside.

"Comfy enough," she whispered, tail flicking.

A distant clang signaled the ramp retracting. The cargo hold rattled as the engines fired to life. Velvet felt the ship rise—slower than the Swift, but strong. Purposeful.

She closed her eyes, satisfied.

But just before sleep tugged at her again, her nose twitched. An unfamiliar scent caught her attention.

Velvet opened one eye, ears twitching.

She wasn't alone in the cargo hold.

CHAPTER VII

Detroit After Dark

Velvet sniffed the air again but she didn't move. Just breathed in slowly, letting the smell roll through her senses. It didn't smell like humans but it didn't smell like food either. She didn't think it was anything mechanical like the rattomatons.

Since she didn't feel any immediate danger, Velvet began to let her guard down a little. Despite still being curled up in the discarded map tube, every muscle was coiled like a spring.

Minutes passed. Then more. It was mostly silent save for the noises made by the Phoenix as it adjusted to the changing altitude. Someone— probably Phineas B. Hagroves—muttered incoherently on the deck above.

But the other presence in the cargo hold never moved.

Eventually, the scent faded.

Velvet stayed awake another hour, just to be

sure. She waited, but nothing came.

Her tail twitched once. Then slowly, she settled deeper into the tube, resting her head on the edge of the wool blanket she had pulled inside.

She yawned and finally dozed off to the soft hum of the steam engines and the occasional creak of wood beneath her.

It was sometime later—a few hours, perhaps—that a very different sound woke her.

Slurp.

Velvet's ears twitched.

Slurp.

She cracked one eye open.

Slurp. Slurp. Gulp.

She sniffed the air.

Stew.

But not just any stew. It was her stew.

Velvet's eyes went wide as she slowly, silently twisted in the map tube and peered out from the edge.

And there it was. Tiny, round-eared, and pink-tailed.

A very small, very white mouse sitting politely in the middle of the cargo hold, hunched over her bowl and slurping from it like it had been properly invited.

Velvet blinked. Then blinked again.

The mouse didn't notice her. It just kept eating, dipping its tiny paws into the edge of the bowl to pull out chunks of meat. It was humming pleasantly to itself.

Velvet's whiskers twitched.

"*Am I still dreaming?*" she thought to herself.

The mouse paused. Its ears twitched. Then, as if sensing her gaze, it looked directly at her.

Its eyes were enormous. And bright.

Velvet stared.

The mouse stared back.

Then it said—very calmly—

"Oh. Hello...."

Velvet blinked again.

The mouse did the same.

Then it started slowly backing away from the bowl.

"Where are you going?" Velvet tilted her head.

"You're a cat aren't you?" He asked nervously.

Velvet began to inch out of the map tube, her muscles tightening. "Last time I checked I was."

Thimble took a few more steps back from the stew. His little paws quivered.

"I didn't mean any harm. I—I just smelled food. I was very hungry and I..."

Velvet lunged!

The bowl clattered as Thimble yelped and darted behind a crate, his tiny claws scrabbling against the floor. Velvet chased him, tail lashing, goggles glinting.

"Thief!" she hissed. "What are you doing

Velvet inched forward and then
Thimble began to move back.

aboard this airship?"

"My name's Thimble! I live here!" he squeaked back, ducking behind a coil of rope.

Velvet pounced over a barrel, missing him by inches as he squeezed through a narrow gap between two crates.

"Don't eat me!" He squeaked pleadingly.

"Eat you?" she snarled. "Don't be ridiculous! Who sent you? Seraphina? The Clockwork Conqueror?"

"No! I'm just a mouse! I used to live in the barn!"

"Barn? What Barn? The Davenport barn?"

"I just called it the barn..."

Velvet froze for a moment.

Thimble saw the opportunity and took advantage of it. He dashed toward a ladder and scurried halfway up before leaping onto a net dangling from the rafters. He remained there, breathless, just out of reach.

"You telling the truth?"

"I swear!" he squeaked. "I used to live in the hay loft with a group of older mice. We had been there for several weeks. That's when they came."

Velvet narrowed her eyes, tail twitching. "They?"

"The metal rats!" Thimble's voice was trembling. "They weren't like us. They were clockwork and had brass tails. Yellow eyes that would change to red when they were angry. They drove us out! Tore up everything! My friends left me behind... they... they said I was too small and would only slow them down."

Velvet's ears flicked.

"You're talking about the Rattomatons."

Thimble nodded quickly, still hanging by a thread. "I've been hiding in here ever since which wasn't easy whenever the humans were working nearby. But I managed to scavenge scraps whenever I could. I never meant to be seen. I didn't even know we were leaving the ground until the floor started moving!"

Velvet hesitated. The little mouse looked half-starved, dangling like a soggy dishrag someone forgot to wring out. No spy would be that pitiful.

She circled below the dangling mouse slowly, assessing.

Finally, Velvet sat down and calmly wrapped her tail around her feet.

"Alright," she said coolly. "You've earned a few seconds of trust."

"Only a few?"

"Don't push it."

"Sorry..."

"Won't you come down now?"

"You won't hurt me?" He squeaked nervously.

"As long as you don't give me a reason to!" She hissed.

Thimble thought about it for a moment then climbed up the net to the rope holding it in place. He immediately slid down to where it was loosely tied to a peg on the wall, inadvertently loosening it.

From there, he leaped to the floor landing with a soft thump. The little mouse stood there nervously, his paws clasped in front of him. "I'm Thimble."

"You've already told me that!" Velvet hissed then immediately softened her tone as she saw how frightened it made him. "My name's Steampunk Velvet but you can call me Velvet.

"Nice to—um—not get eaten by you, Velvet."

"Why do you keep saying that?"

"Because you're a cat and I'm a mouse..."

"That's a negative stereotype!" Velvet hissed as she glanced at the half-empty stew, then back at the tiny mouse. "I only eat what's put in my bowl."

"I'll remember to stay out of your bowl..."

It was at this moment that the rope holding the net in place came completely loose and went crashing to the floor landing directly on top of Velvet. Velvet immediately began to thrash against it and try to twist her way out but the more she fought the more tangled she got.

"You tricked me!" She hissed at Thimble.

"No!" The little white mouse ran towards her not away from her. "I didn't mean for that to happen!"

"Then why am I trapped in here while you're

walking around free?"

"It was an accident!" Thimble pleaded.

Velvet began to calm down realizing she was only making things worse by fighting against it.

"If it was just an accident then you can just find some way to get me out of here!"

The little mouse thought for a moment then opened his mouth wide showing his teeth. "Hold still!" He immediately began chewing through the net one strand at a time until he had freed his feline companion.

The little black cat squirmed loose and then shook herself off. However, instead of saying thank you, she motioned with her head toward the bowl of stew. "You can help yourself to as much as you want but next time ask first."

"Right. Yes. Of course." He turned and raced back over to the food.

Velvet sighed, curled her tail around her paws, and watched the little mouse eat, "We'll figure out what to do with you when we land in Detroit."

Thimble blinked. "Does that mean you're kicking me out?"

"You don't belong here and I'm on an important mission." Velvet patiently waited until he had eaten all he wanted, then she walked over and began finishing the stew.

Saddened Thimble walked away. "Okay. Then... I'll just curl up over here until we land." He looked back at her to see her reaction. "I'll be in this far corner... Way over here... You won't even notice me... Way over here..."

"Good," Velvet said, watching him scurry to a small box and burrow beneath a folded tarp.

She settled back into her map tube, ears still twitching faintly. But as she curled up again, something still itched in the back of her mind. Thimble had been too scared to lie—but maybe not scared enough to tell the whole truth. Either way, she didn't take him as a threat so she yawned and dozed off.

Velvet later briefly woke up as Thimble climbed into the map tube beside her. She instinctively stiffened, ready to hiss him away—until she saw him curled up, snoring softly. She sighed and closed her eyes again.

****

Almost thirteen hours after lifting off from Davenport Ranch, the Phoenix began its graceful descent into Detroit. Below, the city sprawled like a patchwork quilt of flickering gas lamps and glowing shop windows. The river carved a silvery path through the darkness, reflecting the shimmering lights of the industrial hub.

The airship hummed softly, gliding toward an area near the docks—a stark contrast to the bustling noise rising from the streets. The clatter of carriage wheels, the distant shouts of dockworkers, and the low whistle of a train wove together in a symphony of urban life, punctuated by the occasional hiss of steam from nearby factories.

Velvet stirred from her curled-up position in the map tube, blinking against the dim glow filtering through the slats in the cargo bay walls. The scent of coal smoke and damp metal drifted in. They'd landed.

She stretched, slow and deliberate, claws clicking once against the floorboards. The entire ship had quieted, save for the creak of boots overhead and the muted clang of the loading ramp lowering.

Velvet looked back into the tube to see if Thimble was still asleep but she didn't see him. He had gotten up a few minutes before her and was working on something a few feet away.

Velvet ignored whatever he was doing and padded to a porthole to peek out. Her tail twitched as she watched the humans leave the ship headed into the city.

Since nobody was aboard the ship, she found it easy to slip silently out of the cargo hold. The gangplank was still lowered when she bounded down a mooring line and landed with a soft thud on the dock below. No one noticed.

"Hey! Where are you going?" Thimble piped up

behind her. He was dragging Velvet's top hat behind him. It had come off in the net.

Velvet turned to see the little white mouse clambering down the mooring line after her, ears perked, paws gripping the edge.

"Out," she said flatly. "I'm going out and so should you!"

"Wait!" He called after her. "Your hat!"

"Fine..." She trilled as she lowered herself flat and let the mouse pull the hat into place on her head.

"Where are we going?"

"I'm going after my humans... I mean the humans I followed here..." She quickly corrected herself. Even though she was growing more and more protective of Jedidiah, Matthew, and Phineas she wasn't ready to admit it, yet.

Velvet stood up, looked down at Thimble, and hissed. "I don't care where you go as long as you don't come back!"

"But what if you need my help?"

"Your help?" she meowed over her shoulder. "How could a little country mouse like you help me in a big city like this?"

"I know I'm small but I can get in and out of places you can't!"

"Why do you even want to tag along with me?" She hissed.

"You didn't eat me so I figure I owe you!"

"We're even." Velvet meowed. "You rescued me from the net, didn't you?"

"The net that I accidentally dropped on you..."

"If you really want to pay me back, you can do it by getting lost!" Velvet hissed right before she vanished into the fog-drenched streets of Detroit.

The air down here was heavier than she expected. Not with heat, but with tension — something in the steam, the echo, the feel of the cobblestones. Her fur stood on end before her eyes even caught movement.

For the next twenty minutes or so, the little black cat kept to the shadows as she trailed along after the humans. Her ears moved back and forth as the sound of voices echoed off the walls of every building. Her whiskers twitched as her nostrils flared trying to distinguish their scent from the hundreds of others in Detroit that night.

She was just about to give up and head back to the airship when not only did she catch a hint of their scent but she actually spotted all three of them.

Jedidiah Davenport. Matthew Colton. And that puffed-up peacock, Phineas B. Hargroves, as she began to think of him.

They were just ahead, Jedidiah was reading aloud the words on the scroll he held in his hand. That's when Velvet spotted a figure in a plague doctor's cloak, standing motionless at the edge of the shadows. It was one of Lady Seraphina Blackwood's armed guards. Slowly, he raised a gloved hand and beckoned them with a deliberate, almost hypnotic motion.

She watched helplessly as all three stepped into the dimly lit alley.

Then—

Clink.

The distinct sound of a metal ball hitting the cobblestones. A split second later, it erupted into a thick, acrid cloud of smoke. The air filled with the biting stench of sulfur and burnt metal.

Velvet's pupils dilated. Her whiskers flared as she watched all three humans collapse.

"No!" She leapt.

Everything narrowed—her vision, her breath, her focus. She was in mid-leap—

That's when a gray-and-white blur slammed into her from the side—short-furred, muscular, and oddly familiar.

WHAM!

Velvet hit the ground hard, and the wind was almost knocked from her chest. A weight pinned her down.

"What's going on?!" She growled and twisted, trying to free herself.

She finally broke loose and turned to face her attacker. Velvet's claws unsheathed, her ears flat. She was ready to fight—until she saw him.

A cat slightly older than her, judging by the tufting at his ears and the self-important way he held his head. His fur was a blend of white and warm gray-brown, with a tail ringed like a raccoon's and a face marked by sharp tabby stripes.

But that wasn't what made Velvet's eyes narrow or her to hesitate.

What made her pause her attack was the fact that he was wearing a top hat just like hers.

It was the exact same style Lady Blackwood had forced on her months ago. And to make matters more confusing—he had round glasses perched on his nose like he thought he was someone important.

"Hello, Velvet," he purred as if they were old friends.

Velvet arched her back and bared her teeth.

"Who are you and how do you know my name?" she hissed.

The older cat didn't flinch. He simply reached up, adjusted his little top hat with one paw, and gave the faintest, most maddening smile.

"Now now," he said smoothly. "That's no way to greet your big brother."

Velvet froze.

Her ears twitched.

"…Brother?"

"Half-brother, technically," he added, preening as he flicked a speck of dust from his sleeve. "Different litters. Same owner. You really don't know who I am, do you?"

Velvet blinked. "I've never met you. What's your name?"

He took a few slow, deliberate steps toward her.

"Alex," he said, offering a slight bow. "Alex Blackwood, if you want to get formal about it."

Velvet narrowed her eyes. "Blackwood?"

"That's right, I was rescued and taken in by Lady Seraphina, just like you."

"I wasn't rescued," she hissed, not lowering her stance. "I was kidnapped and held against my will!"

He sighed dramatically. "Kidnapped or taken in and cared for?"

"Cared for? I was dressed up like a toy and forced to wear clothes just so I could match her."

"You mean in the outfit you're still wearing?" Alex sat and neatly curled his tail around his feet, then gestured with a tilt of his nose toward her vest, goggles, and identical top hat.

"They're just clothes!" she snapped. "Just because they look good on me doesn't mean I like them."

Velvet's eyes flicked toward the alley.

Her breath caught.

The plague-masked guard was gone.

So were Jed, Matthew, and Phineas.

She spun back toward Alex, eyes blazing.

"You distracted me while that masked thing

made off with MY humans!"

Alex's ears tilted forward, calm as ever. "Relax. They're not hurt."

Velvet arched her back, ready to fight. "You saw what happened to them!"

"I did. But don't worry—they're safe." He raised a paw and casually wiped the side of his face like none of this was urgent. "Seraphina just doesn't like to waste time. She's trying to save the world, after all."

Velvet's tail lashed. "Save the world by knocking people out in alleyways?"

"She didn't knock them out," Alex said with a shrug. "Just a little... sleep vapor. Painless. You know how humans are kinda slow compared to us cats? They can't even understand what we say."

"I've actually met one who can..." Velvet's ear suddenly perked up as she heard a faraway cry for help.

"You did?" Alex stopped bathing his face and looked at her. "A fully grown human?"

There it was again—a faint, high-pitched cry for help. Velvet hissed at him to be quiet while she listened.

"I know some humans can understand us when they're very young but as they get older they all seem to lose the ability..."

Velvet suddenly hissed and showed her teeth again as she growled, "Will you please stop meowing at me?"

"What are you trying to hear?" Alex asked confused. "All I hear is a squeaky voice calling for help. Sounds like a mouse...."

"Thimble!" Velvet hissed in terror.

CHAPTER VIII

Trouble with Thimbles

Velvet spun around as the squeak for help came again.

The cry had come from down the street — distant, high-pitched, unmistakably Thimble.

She bolted.

"Velvet, wait—" Alex meowed as loud as he could.

Too late.

She was already gone.

The narrow alley blurred as she leaped over crates and darted under rusted pipes, the smell of soot and oil thick in her nose. Her claws clicked on the cobblestones as she raced toward the cry.

"Thimble!" she called heart pounding. "Where are you?"

Another squeaky "Help!" rang out — this time from an alley that dead ended behind a closed restaurant.

Velvet skidded to a halt.

She sniffed the ground. Tiny claw marks had scratched the cobblestone. A faint aroma of stew—her stew—led her further behind the building

She crouched low, peering into the dark.

"Thimble?" she whispered.

Silence.

Then—

Clink.

A metallic sound echoed from ahead.

Velvet's ears twitched. That wasn't Thimble.

She took a slow step back.

Out of the darkness came a tiny pair of glowing red eyes.

Velvet's breath caught.

"No," she whispered. "Not here. Not again—"

A Rattomaton emerged from the shadows. But this one was different. Sleeker. Faster. It wasn't wearing a faux fur. Instead, its brass shell was completely exposed etched with swirling sigils and gears that shimmered faintly in the moonlight. In its metal grasp it held a very wriggly, very terrified Thimble.

"Velvet!" the mouse squeaked. "I was coming to help you but this monster grabbed me!"

"I told you I didn't need your help," Velvet growled, sizing up the mechanical rat.

The mechanical rat crouched, steam venting from its sides.

In its metal grasp it held a very
wriggly, very terrified Thimble.

Then it leaped.

Velvet dodged just in time, but the thing spun mid-air and landed behind her with mechanical precision. Its tail whipped around, lashing like a metal whip.

Crack!

Velvet barely ducked it. She rolled and jumped to the side landing in a crouched aggressive position. She bore her teeth and growled.

Still holding Thimble in its metal grip, the metal rodent used the little white mouse for a shield between itself and Velvet.

"Let him go!" Velvet hissed but the steam-driven rodent didn't blink.

She swiped at the rattomaton's legs. Sparks flew as her claws hit metal. It stumbled but didn't fall.

Suddenly three more mechanical rats came running out from a shadow and formed a line between the little black cat and Thimble.

Velvet crouched low and began sizing them up.

From behind, a voice called, "You need a paw?"

Velvet turned and saw a now familiar looking furry figure leaping through the air.

Alex landed beside her, hat tilted, glasses still perfectly in place.

Velvet groaned. "I think I can handle three or four mechanical rats without your help!"

"Three or four?" He quickly motioned with his head. "Look again!"

Velvet turned around just as more skittered from the shadows—first five, then ten. Then too many to count. Before they knew it, they were completely surrounded by dozens of glowing red eyes.

The creature holding Thimble charged again, tail spinning like a blade. Velvet ducked left. Alex dodged right.

"Can I help now?" he asked.

Velvet narrowed her eyes. "Fine. You distract the others while I free the mouse."

"Deal."

Alex lunged with feline grace, swiping at one of the Rattomatons' faces. It screeched in static and reared up. Alex leaped into the air and landed square on the machine's back, and yanked something loose with his teeth.

He bit down hard.

Click.

The metal rat stopped moving.

"Next!" Alex called, as he raced straight at another one.

That was all Velvet needed.

She sprinted straight at the lead antagonist—the one holding Thimble—dodging the others with tight, skidding turns. Her brass goggles bounced against her vest as she launched herself onto its back.

"Let—him—go!" she roared.

She bit into a cable running to both its arms. It

didn't stop it but its grip was forced open.

Thimble tumbled free.

"I got you!" Velvet leaped off the rat and grabbed the little mouse by the scruff of his neck mid-air and twisted in a somersault, landing on all fours. She opened her jaws, and Thimble dropped to the floor, scrambling beneath a pipe.

"Why didn't you get lost like I told you to?" She hissed.

"I just wanted to help," he squeaked from the shadows.

Velvet leaped between him and the main rat. "You can help by going back to the ship!"

"I thought you didn't want me on the ship!"

"I changed my mind!"

Thimble bolted before she had time to change her mind again.

Velvet turned just in time to see three more of the metal rats rushing towards her.

"Alex!" She hissed.

"Little busy!"

He was currently rolling around on the floor with one of the mechanical creatures kicking it with his back feet.

Velvet hissed and stood her ground.

The first Rattomaton lunged—she ducked under its legs and slashed at its belly. A pipe burst, spraying hot steam. The second was faster, trying to flank her. She rolled, then vaulted onto a stack of crates.

"Too slow!" she shouted.

Then the third didn't charge—it fired.

A hiss of compressed air—

Fwwwoosh!

A net shot toward her like a coiled trap.

Velvet turned her head looking for a means of escape but she didn't have time to move out of the way. It was just about to make contact when Thimble came racing back across the floor and leaped between her and the trap.

The net wrapped around him instead, catching his little limbs mid-air and slamming him to the cobblestones.

"Oof!" he groaned, then sprang upright, wobbling, still tangled in the ropes.

"Told you," he declared, grinning through the netting. "You did need my help."

"Wouldn't have needed it—or be in this mess— if it hadn't been for you in the first place!" She hissed turning to face the mechanical opponents.

Undeterred, Thimble dropped to his haunches and started gnawing at the netting.

Alex suddenly appeared beside Velvet, slightly battered but still smug. "Miss me?"

Before Velvet could begin to respond, another mechanical rodent lunged out of the smoke behind them. Alex sprang sideways with a hiss, and the rattomatonhn's snapping metal jaws slammed shut just inches from Velvet's tail.

"No," Velvet finally answered. "But I am glad that thing missed me!"

They backed up until their flanks brushed—Velvet on one side, Alex on the other, both crouched, tails lashing in unison. Thimble behind them still gnawing his way out of the net.

"How many left?" Velvet asked between panting breaths.

"I stopped counting when I ran out of claws." Alex meowed.

"Helpful."

One of the Rattomatons—the one with a cracked lens from one of Velvet's earlier slashes—let out a high-pitched screech and charged again. Velvet sidestepped, letting it crash into the crate behind her. Wood splintered. It stopped moving.

Alex pounced on another that had turned its back. He couldn't tear it apart—he wasn't strong enough—but he bit down on an exposed cable and yanked. The thing screeched and spun in circles, like a dog chasing its own tail.

Velvet took advantage of the distraction and leaped onto a nearby barrel. Her eyes scanned the alley walls. She needed an exit—fast. They couldn't go back the way they came there were too many of them blocking the way.

"Thimble, now's your time!" she called. "Any bright ideas?"

"I've got one…" His voice trailed off as he continued to chew. "Just need two more seconds!"

"We don't have two more seconds!"

Thimble gave one final chomp, and the ropes snapped. The net fell away.

He darted out, tail twitching and eyes wild. "Over there!" he squeaked, pointing with his nose toward a large storm drain grate at the alley's far end.

Velvet's ears twitched. "That's our exit!"

Another Rattomaton skittered toward them, steam hissing from its vents.

"Go!" Velvet hissed. "I'll cover you!"

"I'm small, not fast!" Thimble squeaked, already racing ahead. "Buy me some time!"

Alex darted after him, staying low.

Velvet gave the charging Rattomaton one last hard swipe across the face. Sparks flew. It veered wildly into the wall.

She didn't wait to see if it would recover.

She turned and sprinted after the others, her goggles still bouncing against her vest, while her top hat toppled to the side and rolled across the floor.

Thimble had already reached the grate and squeezed through the bottom, disappearing into the dark.

Alex clawed at the rusted bars.

"Too small!" he hissed. "The holes are only

Thimble size!"

The little mouse stood on the other side looking around trying to figure another way for his friends to join him. Velvet and Alex turned to face the dozens of red glowing eyes coming towards them.

Suddenly, for no apparent reason, the rattomatons stopped advancing. The glow of their eyes flickered—three short pulses, two long—like Morse code. Velvet's ears twitched. Something had changed.

Without warning, the entire swarm turned and retreated into the shadows, vanishing from sight.

"Well," Alex muttered, ears twitching. "That was… strange."

Velvet didn't answer. She kept staring into the mist. Her breathing slowed, but her claws stayed unsheathed. Something about that retreat unsettled her.

Thimble poked his nose back through the grate. "Are they gone?"

"For now," Velvet said, finally blinking. "You okay?"

"This is the most exciting night of my whole mouse life!" He squeaked. "I just got kidnapped, trapped in a net, helped fight a horde of monster rats, and chewed my way to safety, using just my teeth!"

Alex leaned closer to the grate and gave him an assessing look. "You've got courage, I'll give you that."

Velvet growled under her breath. "Too bad he doesn't have the size or strength to back it up."

"Maybe we can fix that," Alex said with a smirk.

"How would..." Velvet flicked her tail sharply, then turned back to the grate. "Never mind, tell me later. We need to get out of this alley. There might be more coming."

"But we can't go through here," Alex said, gesturing with his nose. "We're too big to fit."

"You're right," Velvet groaned. "Guess we'll just have to go back the way we came."

Alex agreed.

"Wait!" Thimble climbed through the grate and raced over to the top hat lying on the ground. He grabbed the brim with his teeth and dragged it back over to Velvet. The little black cat lay down on the floor once more and lowered her head while he brought it to her. This time he got it halfway on, then climbed up on her back and pulled it from behind to put it back in place.

Velvet stood up with Thimble still perched on her shoulders.

"See, I'm helping you all the time now!" He shouted as he grabbed the collar of her vest and held on.

"You're just gonna ride up there?" She hissed.

"Just until we get to where we're going!"

"Thimble..." She meowed gently at first then suddenly hissed. "Get down!"

"Okay..." Thimble hopped off.

The three of them crept back through the alley, climbing over loose bricks and shattered machine parts. Alex kept a lookout behind them. Velvet was just ahead of him. Thimble scurried to the front of the line, sniffing for clear paths like a one-mouse scouting party.

When they emerged into the open street, Velvet's fur was on edge.

The city had changed.

Not the buildings or the lights, but the feeling. The earlier clatter of carriages and hiss of factory vents were fading as it was now much later in the night.

Velvet looked the streets up and down. They were practically empty. She sniffed the air trying to regain the scent of the three men she had followed there.

"What are you doing?" Thimble squeaked.

"I'm trying to find *my* humans!"

"*Your* humans?" Alex meowed.

"Never mind!" She hissed as she took off running.

Velvet darted down the streets of Detroit, her paws pounding the slick stones as Thimble and Alex scrambled to keep up. The buildings loomed around them like crooked giants. Without breaking stride, she leaped onto a tipped-over barrel, then to a stack of crates. From there, she launched herself onto a fire escape, claws scraping metal.

"Wait—where are you going now?" Thimble squeaked, as Alex slowed down enough to let him climb onto his shoulders.

"Up!" Velvet called back without slowing. "The higher I am, the more I can see!"

She scaled the final railing and sprang onto the roof, the city unfolding beneath her like a shadowy patchwork. Something was wrong. She couldn't pick up their scent anywhere. It was like they had vanished. That's when her instincts took over and she decided to keep an eye on a large building that read Detroit Opera House.

The little black cat and her two new friends stayed perched on the roof of the building for what felt like an eternity until finally, Velvet spotted them leaving. Jedidiah Davenport, Matthew Colton, and Phineas B. Hargroves.

Making their way back to the streets below them, the three gave chase one more time.

"They're going back to the docks!" Velvet meowed. "I can smell the fish from here!"

That's when she heard it

The faint hum of distant engines.

Velvet turned sharply, eyes wide.

"No—no no no—"

She scrambled up the side of a nearby

warehouse, raced to the roof's edge, and scanned the skyline. Fog swirled in ribbons. Smokestacks rose around her like towers. And far above, just visible through the haze, the Phoenix was lifting off.

The sleek wooden hull with its brass accents gleamed in the moonlight as it rose, slow but steady.

"They're leaving," Velvet said, stunned. Her ears drooped slightly. "I was so close..." she murmured, more to herself than the others.

Alex trotted up beside her and stared at the sky. "Is that your airship flying away?" He meowed.

"It's not my airship!" Velvet snapped. "It belongs to my humans... I mean to the humans I've been trying to find."

Thimble, still holding onto Alex's fur, and breathing hard, asked. "Does this mean we're stranded?"

"I hate to admit this..." Velvet's voice dropped to a whisper. "But yeah. We're stuck." Her tail drooped, brushing the rooftop like a fallen flag.

CHAPTER IX

Nevermore

Velvet stood there, chest heaving, tail rigid, goggles dangling around her neck.

The airship rose higher and higher until it disappeared in the night sky, and the last sound Velvet heard was the soft, rising pulse of its steam core as it sailed away.

The Phoenix was gone.

Thimble climbed down from Alex's back, chewing nervously on a piece of net he still had stuck in his teeth. "So… what now?"

Velvet didn't answer. She just stared into the sky a moment longer.

Then, slowly, she turned her back to the horizon.

"We find them," she said, her voice low but steady. "No matter what or how long it takes."

She swatted at her goggles with one of her paws until they were straight, turned, and started climbing down the side of the building.

Thimble climbed back onto Alex's shoulders and the two of them followed Velvet down the side of the building with graceful ease, landing beside her with a soft thump. Alex's hat barely shifted.

"You've got that look again," he said, brushing against the side of the building to remove some dust.

"What look?"

"The, *I'm about about to bite someone*, look."

"I might," Velvet replied. "Just not sure who."

Thimble's eyes widened and he buried his face into Alex's fur.

"Not you!" Velvet hissed.

"Phewww!" The little mouse flopped backward and almost slid off.

"I guess now we need to find a new airship," Velvet mused.

"We don't need a new one," Alex said, ears twitching. "Just a different one."

"A different one?" Velvet's ears perked up.

Alex gave a sly smile, as much as a cat can smile. "I know where there's another one not far from here." He tipped his head toward the towering silhouette of the Detroit Opera House, barely visible through the haze. "Belongs to a mutual friend of ours."

Velvet ears laid back.

Her pupils narrowed.

"You mean..."

Alex nodded. "Lady Seraphina Blackwood. I'm sure she's still inside that building. I haven't smelled her come out yet."

"She's here?" Velvet's voice dropped an octave. "Right now?"

Alex shrugged. "Missed her?"

Velvet looked away, her fur bristling.

"Her ship was my prison," she said quietly.

"Right," Alex said. "And now, it's your ride."

"No," Velvet said, shaking her head so hard she almost knocked her hat off. "I won't do it!"

"It's the only way!" Alex purred.

Thimble glanced between them. "I don't understand. What's the big deal about this airship?"

Velvet took a deep breath and began to tell Thimble everything that had happened.

****

Meanwhile, as Thimble was listening intently to Velvet's story, back at The Davenport ranch, the two little cats known as Dottie and Panther were lounging peacefully in the barn.

Dottie sat perched on what was once a very respectable high-backed armchair. Now, its stuffing stuck out in patches, one leg was slightly cracked, and it smelled faintly of machine oil, hay, and victory.

Panther lounged on the matching settee — upside down, paws in the air, head hanging off the edge.

"I wonder what Velvet is up to," Dottie purred, clawing a bit more stuffing loose from the armrest.

Panther stretched and rolled off the settee. He landed on the dirt floor. "Did she go somewhere?"

His claws extended and retracted lazily as he scratched long grooves into a wooden furniture leg.

"Don't you remember?" Dottie flipped over onto her side and started rubbing her back against the seat cushion. "She left early this morning!"

"Is that a long time?"

"Are you kidding?" Dottie stopped rolling around and looked down at him. "Do you know how many times we've eaten and napped since she left? She's been gone forever!"

"I lose track of time when it comes to food and naps..." He yawned as though he was about to drift off again.

Just then, the barn doors creaked open.

Both cats froze.

A lantern's soft glow spilled across the floor as Pat Bennington stepped inside, holding a half-eaten sandwich in one hand and a bowl of tuna in the other.

"Jed is gonna have a come apart when he sees the condition of his furniture," he muttered. "He won it at the county fair, you know."

Dottie sat upright. "It wasn't us!" Chair stuffing lay all around her.

"Don't play innocent with me," he laughed as he sat the bowl down. "I know it was the two of you and Velvet. Now who's up for a midnight snack?"

Panther immediately sprang up from the floor, raced over, and plopped his face down in the bowl.

Pat leaned back against the wall, sandwich nearly gone.

"You know, there was a time I thought I'd settle down somewhere, build me a little place of my own with a wraparound porch. Maybe a couple of goats. Then I met Jed."

Dottie blinked. "Is he… telling us his life story?"

"He is," Panther whispered between bites.

"Didn't ask for it."

"Doesn't matter."

"He practically begged me to come work for him. Said he couldn't find a decent cook this side of Wichita." Pat let out a satisfied sigh and polished off the last of his sandwich. "Still think about that place of my own sometimes. Porch. Goats. Maybe a peach tree."

He brushed crumbs from his shirt and stuck his thumbs behind his suspenders, then froze.

A soft clang echoed from the far side of the barn.

All three heads turned.

Dottie's ears twitched. Panther froze mid-lick.

"What was that?" Pat said quietly.

Another sound — a hiss this time. Faint. Metallic. Like steam being released in the wrong place.

Pat slowly stood. "That better not be another one of them masked intruders."

Panther crouched low to the ground. "Do they go clank?"

The lantern on the wall flickered as Pat stepped forward. "Now hold on... who or what's out there?"

Another hiss. This one was closer than the last.

"Okay," Pat said, backing up a step. "I guess they just want to stay unanimous."

"Anonymous," Dottie hissed.

There was another metal clank even closer now.

Panther ducked behind the settee. "I vote we hide behind the goats."

"There are no goats," Dottie whispered.

"What happened to them?" Panther's eyes widened. "Is that what's been in the stew?"

Pat Bennington, crouching behind the settee with Panther, raised his head and peeked over.

"Now it's okay if whoever or whatever you are don't wanna reveal yourself," he said. "We're perfectly fine with you remaining magnanimous!"

"Anonymous!" Dottie growled.

"Shush!" Panther hissed. "I think I hear something!" His ears perked up.

For a moment all remained quiet. Suddenly, a sharp caw shattered the silence.

Not the kind of caw you heard in the trees—this one was raspy, slightly distorted like it had flown through a thunderstorm and swallowed a wrench.

All three heads snapped upward.

A shape flew through the hay loft and dropped from the rafters, half-silhouette, half-nightmare. Black feathers glinted with strips of tarnished copper, and along its spine, tiny gears clicked and spun with each breath. One wing beat silently; the other gave a soft metallic creak, tiny pistons hissing with every motion. A round monocle that glowed red attached to its face.

"WHAT," the crow shrieked, voice guttural and almost mechanical, "HAPPENED TO THE RATTOMATONS?"

Panther's ears flattened. "Another machine?"

"No..." Dottie sprang to the top of the armchair. "This bird is real. I can smell it from here!"

The crow banked hard, circling the rafters with unnatural speed, the mechanical wing stuttering with each turn. Its organic eye burned yellow with fury; the other flickered red like a signal light.

It dropped lower, scanning the debris piled up in buckets along the wall. Bits of broken gears, tails, whiskers.

The crow flapped once and landed with a clank-thud on a broken beam.

"RATTOMATONS," it repeated, pacing with a twitchy, birdlike strut. "GONE. ALL GONE. DESTROYED. BY WHO?"

Suddenly, without warning, Dottie leaped from the chair trying to reach the odd bird.

The crow launched upward in a burst of steam, spiraling toward the loft before she hit the ground.

"TOO SLOW!" it mocked in a harsh caw. "CATS ARE TOO SLOW!"

Panther crouched, eyes narrowed. "Come down here and say that to our faces!"

In acceptance of the challenge, the crow swooped down and the sleek muscular cat lunged at it just as it skimmed past a stack of crates. For half a second, Panther had it in his claws, but the bird twisted midair and shot up like a bolt of lightning.

"Agh! Almost!" Panther hissed, landing in their water bowl, and splashing water all over himself and the floor.

The crow darted through a gap in the rafters and perched upside down from a support beam, like a deranged bat.

"BRASSWELL WON'T LIKE THIS," it croaked. "YOU WILL ALL PAY!"

Dottie's fur bristled as she growled. "Did it just say Brasswell?"

"It did!" Panther hissed.

"Who's that?"

"I don't know!"

"What's it saying?" Pat asked, blinking hard like he wasn't sure if he was hallucinating. "Who's Brasswell?"

"Can't you understand it?" Panther trotted up next to his sister, dripping wet, not even looking back at the rotund man. "I thought you could talk to animals!"

"Sorry," he chuckled. "I'm not fluent in crow."

"YOU WILL PAY," the half bird half machine repeatedly cawed, "YOU WILL ALL PAY!"

Panther bristled. "Okay, now it's just taunting us!"

"BRASSWELL WON'T BE PLEASED. WON'T BE PLEASED AT ALL."

It dove again.

Dottie and Panther anticipated this and both sprang in perfect coordinated harmony.

However, they both missed.

The crow whooshed past, knocking over the half-empty tuna bowl with a clang, then zipped out the open hayloft in a rush of air and steam.

The barn fell quiet again.

Pat stood slowly. "Well… at least we're all still in one piece!"

Just as he said this, the crow flew back in, swooped down, and grabbed Pat's bowler off his head. He gripped the brim in his talons and flew back out.

Dottie and Pather sprang at the crow
in perfect coordinated harmony.

"My hat!" Pat exclaimed as though he'd just lost an old friend.

Panther blinked. "Did that bird just—?"

"Steal my hat?" Pat clutched his head like he'd lost a limb. "It sure did! That was a genuine derby! I bought it from a respectable street vendor down an alley in Kansas City!"

"What did it want?" Dottie asked still looking up at the ceiling.

"A buck seventy-five!" Pat announced proudly.

"The crow!" Dottie hissed. "Not the vendor!"

"Oh yeah," Pat chuckled slightly embarrassed. "But speaking of my hat. The very same one was selling down the street for three dollars..."

"Pat!" Panther meowed loudly.

"Oh, sorry," the rotund man tugged at his suspenders. "I won't bring it up again."

"Good," Dottie meowed.

"Not even if you beg me!"

"Great!"

"Not even if you offered to hunt that bird down and bring back my hat!" He thought about it for a moment. "Actually if you did that I might tell you the whole story after all. It was right before I started working for Jed..."

"Pat!" Dottie and Panther both meowed in unison.

Dottie ran over to a wooden post and raised up on it. Not able to resist her instincts she quickly sharpened her claws on it before she began climbing it. "That crow's working for someone. You heard what it said—Brasswell!"

"Are you sure it wasn't just one of those words birds randomly say, like *crackers* or *nevermore*?" Panther offered.

Dottie shook her head. "No. That name meant something. It came here specifically to check on those rattomatons. It was furious when it discovered they'd been destroyed. You heard it say, you will all pay!"

"Wait a second!" Pat gulped. "Did you just say it said you will *all* pay?"

"Yes, why?"

"Do you think that it includes me as part of you all?" Pat asked nervously.

"Don't worry," Panther walked over and started weaving around the rotund man's leg. This was partly to comfort Pat Bennington but mostly to dry himself off. "We'll protect you!" He meowed.

"Thanks," Pat smiled but then furrowed his brow. "So, this Brasswell fellow sent those mechanical rodents and the crow? That means he's got machines both on the ground and in the sky."

Panther looked around nervously. "You think there's more crows?"

Dottie narrowed her eyes. "Or worse. Falcons."

"Maybe even a few owls!" Pat added.

The three of them went quiet.

Finally, Pat Bennington straightened up and brushed off his shirt. "Alright. That does it. I'm riding into town first thing in the morning and reporting this to Sheriff Thompson."

Panther tilted his head. "What are you gonna say? I was in the barn talking to my two best friends who just happen to be cats when a half crow half machine swooped in, tried to kill us, and stole my hat?"

"Of course not, I'm not stupid," Pat said as he made his way toward the barn doors. "I'll mention my hat first."

"Pat!" Dottie ran over to him, reared up on his pants leg, and dug her claws in to stop him. "You can't go! They'll lock you up if you tell them you talk to cats!"

"Which is why I won't tell the sheriff that part," he said, tapping his temple. "I'll tell him the two of you were talking to me and I was just listening, trying not to be rude..."

Dottie sighed as she flopped onto her side and covered her face with both front paws.

****

Meanwhile, as Dottie, Panther, and Pat Bennington were deciding what to do next, back in Detroit, Velvet, Alex, and Thimble were busy working on sneaking aboard the Aetherwind.

Velvet crouched low beside a pile of broken bricks, her fur prickling with tension. Thick smoke clung to the air like a bad memory. The remains of an old foundry loomed around them, walls blackened by soot, chimneys gutted and silent. Rusted gears and discarded iron piping lay scattered like bones from a long-dead machine.

Ahead, The Aetherwind hovered in near silence, tethered above the broken courtyard. Its hull gleamed faintly in the moonlight, casting crooked shadows through the collapsed roof beams. The ship's mooring lines were looped through what was once a crane gantry, its arms outstretched like a prehistoric skeleton.

Velvet's goggles glinted as she peered between the weeds.

"That's it," she whispered. "I can smell the lavender and wood smoke from here."

Alex lay beside her, his golden eyes catching the faint light. Thimble crouched behind a barrel full of old nails, chewing his claws nervously. "I thought we'd be on board by now. This feels like a slow march to doom."

"Sorry if I'm not in a rush to return to my prison," Velvet murmured.

"You still feel like you were being kept as a prisoner?" Alex meowed casually.

"She wouldn't let me come and go as I wanted, she kept me inside, forced me to eat what she called gourmet food all the time," Velvet said, "What would you call that?"

"Being well fed and well taken care of," Alex meowed almost resentful.

"If it was so great, why did you run away?" Velvet hissed as she turned to face her older brother.

"I didn't run away!" he hissed. "She gave me away..."

"Gave you away?" Velvet's ears flicked back and her brow furrowed. "Why would she do that?"

"She said she wanted a cat that looked more like her. Your black fur and green eyes perfectly matched her own. So she gave me to one of her friends. He was taking me away, the day her guards brought you on the ship."

Velvet didn't respond at first. Her tail flicked, the tip twitching with unspoken emotion.

"I didn't know," she said finally. "I didn't even see you that day."

Alex gave a soft huff. "You were too busy trying to get away."

Before Velvet could answer, Thimble's nose twitched.

"Uh… I don't want to interrupt this touching moment," he whispered, whiskers still twitching, "but…"

He pointed with a trembling paw. Two of Seraphina's guards were approaching the airship, their plague masks glinting in the moonlight.

And there she was. Lady Seraphina Blackwood. Tall, poised, unmistakable — with two more guards flanking her like shadows.

"What now?" Velvet asked stunned.

"You still want to get aboard that ship?" Alex meowed urgently.

"I don't want to... I have to..."

Not waiting for her to finish her sentence, Alex let out a loud trill. This caught the attention of the two guards on the right side of the formation. They turned and looked directly at Velvet.

As they were approaching, the gray-and-white cat grabbed Thimble by the scruff of his neck with his teeth and scrambled off.

Velvet crouched, ready to spring—then blinked.

She suddenly realized that Alex and Thimble were no longer beside her.

A heavy arm grabbed her from behind. She yowled, claws flashing, but it was too late.

The world went dark once again as she was lowered into a burlap sack.

CHAPTER X

Back in Captivity

With Velvet neatly stowed aboard The Aetherwind, the airship lifted from the earth like a dream uncoiling and ascending into the night sky.

Above the ruins of the foundry, its pristine white envelope shimmered against the moonlight, blue motifs swirling like lace in a sky of ash. Silver bands along its hull caught the glow of distant city lights, casting flickers across the blackened brick. The crystal rotors spun with a quiet hum—too soft, too perfect.

On a rooftop just beyond the mooring yard, Alex crouched low behind the remnants of a shattered smokestack. His golden eyes tracked the ship as it rose in a slow, elegant arc. Steam and crystal light mingled beneath it, sending fractured reflections skimming across the rooftops.

Suddenly, something small and quite furious kicked him in the chest.

"Let! Me! Go!"

Thimble squirmed wildly, paws thrashing. His fur stood on end like he'd been shocked, and his whiskers twitched with rage. Alex held him delicately by the scruff of the neck, jaw tight.

With a sigh, he set the mouse down.

Thimble tumbled across the rooftop and immediately sprang up, spinning to face him.

"You betrayed her!" he shouted, his tiny voice slicing through the night. "She trusted you, and you let them take her!"

"I was helping her," Alex said flatly.

"Helping her?" Thimble's ears flattened. "By letting them put her in a bag and drag her back to the floating nightmare palace she escaped from?!"

"They were about to leave," Alex's gaze never left the sky. "She had to get aboard that ship so she could find her humans."

"You should have let her make her own decision." Thimble's little claws clenched. "You... you didn't even warn her! You just grabbed me and ran!"

Alex flicked one ear but didn't reply.

The Aetherwind gained altitude, drifting with uncanny grace, stabilizer fins adjusting in minute increments. The observation deck gleamed as it passed through a shaft of moonlight, like a glass crown on a silver ghost. Along the bottom of the gondola, the compass rose emblem glinted—crystal coil twined with gold.

Thimble's voice cracked. "She's my best friend and I'll never see her again."

"I wouldn't say that," Alex murmured.

Thimble's tail lashed. "What do you mean?"

Alex turned, eyes hard. "Because we're going after her."

Thimble stood on tiptoe and pointed a trembling paw at the now-distant ship. "How? She's gone and we don't have an airship."

"No." Alex stood slowly, tail flicking like a metronome of tension. "But my new owner does and I have a feeling he's going to the same place she is."

Thimble blinked. "A feeling?"

"Just trust me," his voice lowered as he crouched down. "Climb on my back and I'll prove it to you."

"Trust you?" Thimble stared at him. "After what you just did?"

"Well, you don't have to trust me," Alex said, low. "But I'm all you've got. So you can either stay here or you can come with me."

Thimble's whiskers twitched. "I'm going to regret this," he muttered as he scrambled up.

As he was climbing up onto the grey and white cat's shoulders, the last glint of the airship vanished into the haze above, leaving only silence and the faint scent of lavender and smoke.

"Hold tight!" Alex meowed as he stood and without further warning took off at a full run.

****

Sometime later, Velvet's ears began to twitch as she slowly came to, the faint hum of crystal rotors reverberating through the floor beneath her. She was lying on something soft—velvet, perhaps, though that felt too ironic. Satin! It was her familiar red satin pillow!

Her paws flexed against it instinctively, testing for resistance, for balance, for leverage. The texture confirmed what she already knew, she was back aboard Lady Blackwood's airship.

A faint vibration in the air told her she was no longer grounded. The engine's resonance was smooth and very familiar. She could tell by the gentle swaying of the room she was airborne.

Her vision sharpened as her eyes adjusted to the dim light. She wasn't in a cage as she feared she would be. At least not a traditional one.

She was back in a very familiar looking private chamber. Polished hardwood floors, and intricate brass sconces along the walls glowing with soft crystal light. A single arched window curved into the shape of a teardrop, its glass so polished she could see her reflection in it. Beyond that, moonlight shimmered across a sea of clouds.

Velvet pushed herself to her feet, tail low, nose twitching. She could still smell the tranquilizer—faint but unmistakable. The bag she had been tossed in must have been dipped in it.

A soft clink made her freeze.

She turned her head. A white porcelain dish sat a few feet away, beside a small bowl of water. Poached salmon, cooled but fresh.

She blinked.

The door across the room hissed closed and a moment later reopened.

Lady Seraphina Blackwood swept into the room with the quiet force of a storm contained in silk and brass. Her black velvet cloak, fastened with silver clasps, flared dramatically behind her like a shadow. A high collar framed her sharp jawline, and a corseted bodice of layered brocade hinted at elegance forged for battle. Her gloved hands were folded neatly at her waist. The polished leather of her boots clicked against the floor as she crossed thé room, her presence enough to silence even the crackling hearth. When Lady Blackwood entered a room, she didn't just enter—she owned it.

"You're awake," she said, in that calm, melodic voice that always sounded polite but mysterious at the same time.

Velvet didn't respond. She simply stared.

Seraphina's lips curved faintly. "I'm glad to have you back on board."

She moved to the curved settee against the wall and lowered herself with effortless grace, her posture straight, every motion deliberate. Crossing one leg smoothly over the other, she adjusted the fall of her cloak with a flick of her fingers.

"I am, admittedly, curious," she said, her voice cool and composed. "Where exactly have you been —and how did you manage to find your way to Detroit?"

Velvet growled low in her throat.

"No need for theatrics," Lady Blackwood replied, her tone unbothered. "You're not a prisoner. If you'd rather fling yourself out the observation window, or off the deck railing, I won't stop you."

Velvet's glanced at the ornate glass window. She darted over and stood up on her hind legs to look out.

They were thousands of feet above the ground.

Seraphina remained seated, spine perfectly straight, her gloved hands folded lightly in her lap. "Velvet, I realize you can't understand me. You simply lack the mental capacity."

"I understand everything, Lady." Velvet hissed. "You're just too arrogant to notice."

"We are currently on a very important mission," she trailed off, watching the little black cat closely, "...the fate of the entire world is in our hands."

That got a reaction.

Velvet's tail twitched, and her ears angled

forward just slightly.

Lady Blackwood studied the little cat's face. A flicker of something unreadable crossed her own. "*Impossible,*" she murmured inwardly. "*She's just a cat.*" And yet, for a moment, she wasn't entirely certain. "*Did she just understand what I said?*" But she quickly dismissed the idea.

Seraphina exhaled softly, smoothing the edge of her cloak. "You couldn't possibly realize what's at stake," she said aloud, her voice softer now, almost reflective. "The world as we know it has the possibility of unraveling—thread by thread."

She paused to once again study Velvet's reaction but this time Velvet didn't respond in any way.

"Oh never mind," Seraphina stood, smoothed her cloak, and turned toward the door.

"When this is over," she said quietly, "you'll understand why you need to be by my side."

She paused in the doorway, her silhouette etched in crystal-blue light.

"For now… eat. We have far to go, and I'd prefer you not to pass out from hunger."

The door hissed shut behind her, leaving Velvet alone with the hum of rotors.

With nothing else to do, Velvet decided to re-familiarize herself with the room. Everything was mostly the same except for a large painting that caught her eye. It was partially hidden behind a velvet curtain.

Curious, she padded over and batted the curtain aside with one paw.

Her breath caught.

It was a portrait—of her.

Life-sized, framed in brass, painted with obsessive precision. There she was, sitting atop a stylized gear, dressed to the nines in her top hat, vest, and goggles, fur practically gleaming. Her green eyes were intense. Regal. Almost smug.

But the patch of white fur on her chest...

"Oh come on," she muttered. "It's not that big."

She sat back and huffed. "And with my vest on, you can barely even see it."

Velvet tilted her head, studying the rest. The artist had definitely captured her heroic nature.

She narrowed her eyes.

It went perfectly with the portrait of Lady Blackwood over the mantle. Velvet looked back and forth between the two paintings.

"*This must've been what she was doing when she kept sketching me without asking... I thought she was measuring me for a new vest.*" She purred. "*But that circus tent background only reinforces my original opinion of this outfit.*"

After a moment, Velvet turned and walked away.

****

Early the next morning, Sunday, October 23rd, 1881, the sky above Toronto was washed in pale gold and morning mist. A field on the city's edge stretched out like a forgotten postcard—long grasses bending in the breeze, distant rooftops just visible over the trees.

The Aetherwind sat moored at the far end of the field, its hull gleaming dully under the sun's slow rise. There was no grand fanfare. No guards patrolling, no clamor of docking equipment—just stillness and the low, steady churn of the ship's crystal core.

Lady Seraphina Blackwood stood at the forward deck rail, gloved hands resting lightly on the polished brass. Her gaze was tilted skyward, unreadable. The breeze played with the edge of her cloak, and a single strand of dark hair had slipped free from her pin-tight style—but she made no move to fix it.

Velvet padded across the deck, her paws making no sound. She hopped onto the railing beside Seraphina, her tail curling around the wrought iron baluster as she balanced there, ears angled toward the wind.

They stood in silence, the two of them—woman and cat—watching the sky.

Then, on the horizon, a flicker of movement.

Velvet's breath caught.

The Phoenix.

It broke from the clouds, sunlight gleaming across it. The sight of it sent a jolt through her chest.

She tensed, muscles coiling instinctively.

Her claws gripped the railing.

She wanted to leap, but the airship was too far. Already sweeping past. Its engines hummed like a memory, fading before her eyes.

Velvet's tail lowered.

"Finally!" Seraphina didn't look away. "They're finally on their way again toward Lake Simcoe," she murmured, more to herself than to anyone else. "Why the detour?"

Velvet didn't answer. Lady Blackwood wouldn't have understood if she had.

A quiet rustle of boots interrupted the silence. One of the guards stepped onto the deck and approached.

He held out a small rolled-up piece of paper.

Seraphina took it without a word. She read it over.

Her jaw tightened.

"So that's why they stopped off in Toronto," she said coldly. "He sent something from the telegraph office. I want to know what it was."

She turned abruptly toward the stairs, already

striding away. "Stay with the ship," she called over her shoulder to the guard. "And keep her inside. No wandering."

The masked guard merely bowed.

Velvet's ears twitched. She jumped down from the rail and padded after her—but Seraphina was already descending the loading plank, two guards following in her wake.

Velvet sat on the deck alone, the wind teasing through her fur.

The Phoenix was gone again.

She remained motionless long after the footsteps had faded away.

Turning back she padded her way across the ship. The door to Seraphina's quarters was just slightly ajar. Velvet paused. Her nose twitched. She went back inside.

The door whispered shut behind her.

Constantly under surveillance, Velvet had not had a chance to properly search the place. With Seraphina away again, now was her chance.

She moved carefully across the chamber, claws sheathed, ears angled for the smallest sound. The room remained quiet—crystal sconces glowing in low warmth, polished brass fixtures gleaming faintly. The porcelain dish refilled with fresh salmon sat beside the water bowl.

She ignored it.

Her eyes settled on the drafting table. She rose

on her hind legs a few times, judging the height, then leaped up on it.

Once again she spotted the plans for the thing she had heard Lady Blackwood refer to as the chronomechanism. That's when she spotted a whole other set of plans. She leaned in close and sniffed them.

"This would be so much easier if I could read..." she thought to herself as she lifted her head and curled her top lip as though she just smelled something sour.

Even though she couldn't decipher what was written on the paper, she could get an idea from the sketches accompanying the words. It showed various small animals decked out in what looked like metal armor with gears and cogs embedded in them. There were birds, dogs, cats, and even mice.

Velvet sniffed the drawing of the cat and then hopped off the table. She raced across the room to the full-length mirror and looked at herself. Her top hat was still in place. Her goggles were resting up on the brim and her vest looked immaculate. But that wasn't what she was investigating.

"I think that was me..." She turned and went back to the table. After hopping back up she looked at it more closely. "That *is* me!"

Velvet immediately began pushing the paper with her nose rolling it up as she walked along the table. A moment later the scroll fell off and hit the

For just that instant, she forgot she was
on a mission. She forgot Seraphina.
She forgot the threat of the world.
She was just a cat again.

floor. That's when she leaped off and pounced on it.

She rolled around on the floor for a moment, front legs locked around it while her back paws battered it in a flurry of kicks. For just that instant, she forgot she was on a mission. She forgot Seraphina. She forgot the threat of the world unraveling thread by thread.

She was just a cat again.

Velvet's purring started low and involuntary. Her eyes fluttered half-closed as she clutched the paper like prey.

Then—a sound.

The mechanical hiss of the door opening.

Velvet released the scroll and flipped over onto all fours. She padded her way soundlessly underneath the large canopy bed. Her eyes narrowed. Muscles tensed.

Someone was about to enter and it didn't smell like Seraphina or the guards.

A faint shimmer of blue light flickered across the room. Gears ticked in perfect rhythm.

Then the shape emerged—tall, gleaming, inhuman.

A chill swept over her as the masked face of the Clockwork Conqueror appeared.

CHAPTER XI

Clockwork Reckoning

Velvet held her breath beneath the canopy bed, every muscle pulled taut as piano wire. The Clockwork Conqueror stepped deeper into the chamber, gears in his mechanical arm ticking like a distant metronome. His eyes—or lenses, or whatever they were—swept the room in a slow, searching arc.

And then… he stopped. He reached up and removed the brass mask from his face and slipped his goggles down around his neck.

Velvet's pupils narrowed. Her ears flattened. She had absolutely no idea who he really was under the mask, but would definitely recognize him if she ever saw him again.

That's when the Conqueror spotted his wanted poster tacked to the wall across from him. The letter opener was still lodged between his brass goggles. He started to remove it but changed his mind. He seemed to have more important things to attend to.

"What did she do with my designs!" he muttered, voice edged with fury, as he moved straight to the drafting table, boots clicking sharply on the floorboards. As he passed, his foot bumped the scroll that had fallen off. He never even glanced down. It spun lazily across the floor and came to rest just inches from the bed skirt—close enough for Velvet to reach out and snag with her paw.

"What could she possibly want with those augment schematics..." he muttered, trailing off. "Wait—what's this?"

On the table, he spotted her copy of the blueprints for the chronomechanism. "So she's after the device as well..."

As he looked the plans over, Velvet's paw shot out. One swat. Two. She caught the edge of the scroll on the third try and dragged it beneath the bed.

The moment the Conqueror leaned in for a closer look at the blueprints on the table, a faint hum charged the air—then a bolt of searing blue light tore past his head and slammed into the far wall with a concussive crack. Gilded wallpaper and splinters of wood burst outward in a shower of scorched debris.

The Clockwork Conqueror instinctively recoiled, ducking low behind the drafting table. He jerked his mask back on and yanked the goggles over his eyes.

Velvet's eyes widened as she retreated further under the bed.

In the smoke and sudden silence, a shadow appeared in the doorway. One of the guards in complete plague doctor attire as always stepped inside. The barrel of an atomic blaster rifle gleamed in the low crystal light, still glowing faintly from the shot.

It wasn't clear if it had been a warning shot or a misfire. Either way, she didn't care. She stayed frozen beneath the bed, paws pressed to the scroll.

The guard took another step into the room. The blaster remained trained, unwavering.

Then there was the sound of more footsteps as the second guard appeared in the doorway, silhouetted in the blue haze. He was brandishing another rifle.

This guard entered without a word, flanking the first. Together, they raised their weapons.

"Stand down," they said in unison, voices eerily synced through the mask's filtered distortion.

The Conqueror stilled.

Velvet's ears flattened at the strange chorus of their demand. She tucked herself even tighter beneath the bed frame, still clinging to the scroll, tail coiled around her side.

"Surrender now," one of the guards added.

"I disagree," the Conqueror said calmly, his metal arm inching toward the tesla rod attached to his side.

"You're not authorized to be aboard this vessel," the other guard added. "Surrender and we'll let you live."

The Conqueror tilted his head slightly.

"What's my second option?" he asked, voice like grinding steel.

The silence stretched. Neither guard moved.

The Conqueror moved fast. His metal arm jerked sideways—gripping the handle of the lightning rod.

A surge of blue current hissed through the power cable running from the rod to the humming pack on his back. The tip flared with crackling energy.

He swung the weapon upward and fired.

A bolt of blazing electricity lanced across the room—but the guards had already moved.

The blast struck the drafting table instead, vaporizing the edge and searing a black scorch mark across the chronomechanism blueprints.

One of the guards fired in return, the atomic blast punching into the ceiling. The second aimed lower.

The bolt smashed directly into the arched observation window—glass exploded outward with a thunderous crack.

Despite being moored close to the ground, a strong gust of wind tore through the chamber in a howling rush.

The Conqueror kicked the drafting table hard— flipping it into the line of fire. Papers scattered and both guards jerked back instinctively.

In that blink of hesitation, he sprang forward and dove cleanly through the shattered window.

"Fools," he muttered as he hit the ground running.

****

Meanwhile, on the deck of another airship—a vessel known only by the brass plate bolted to its side, The Obsidian—Alex prowled a narrow corridor, with Thimble clinging between his shoulders, claws tucked tightly into his fur. The ship vibrated gently beneath their feet.

The interior of the Obsidian was a far cry from the Aetherwind. It smelled faintly of machine oil, aged teakwood, and something sweet—cardamom, maybe. The gears didn't purr so much as they rattled, and every polished surface was just slightly mismatched, as though the ship had been cobbled together.

"Are you sure this is a good idea?" Thimble whispered near Alex's ear.

"No," Alex replied flatly, "but I don't see you

suggesting anything better."

Thimble gave a tiny groan and slumped down, tail draping between Alex's shoulder blades. "If we don't make it off of this floating patchwork disaster, I'm going to haunt you."

"Just promise me one thing." Alex tilted his head towards the little mouse.

"What?"

"When we're both ghosts you'll learn to float on your own and not ride my shoulders for eternity!"

Thimble thought for a moment, whiskers twitching before blurting out, "No promises!"

They passed through a door that hissed softly open and entered a private chamber. This one was far less fancy than Lady Blackwood's. It was filled with mechanical parts and schematics. More like a workshop than a private suite.

"This is where I live with my new human," Alex announced.

He was just now giving Thimble a tour of the airship because after they had snuck aboard Thimble had spent the entire night hidden in the cargo hold. After flying for hours, the owner of the Obsidian had landed the airship and gone on an errand.

Alex leaped up onto the worktable, paws light on the scattered blueprints.

Thimble squinted down at one of the diagrams. His face lit up as he slid down from Alex's back.

"So much paper!" He exclaimed. "I can make me a good nest with all this!"

Alex's tail flicked. "I wouldn't."

"Why not?" The little mouse was already sinking his teeth into the corner of one blueprint. He stopped and looked back at his feline friend.

"For some reason, they're very important to my human."

"I hear what you're saying, but... paper!"

"Just trust me," Alex sat down and began grooming himself. "You don't want to upset my human."

Suddenly a distant thud echoed through the corridor—followed by the rhythmic thud of heavy boots.

Thimble whipped his head toward the door. "Did you hear that?"

"Hide!" Alex hissed as he bolted up.

The little mouse darted behind a half-dismantled pressure engine just as the door slid open with a mechanical sigh.

It was at this moment that the Clockwork Conqueror stepped inside.

He moved with purpose, tearing the mask from his face and throwing it onto the desk.

"Ignorant fools," he muttered. "Two armed guards stood in my way and prevented me from retrieving my schematics!"

He turned and looked at the little cat in the top

hat and spectacles. Alex tried to act casual, grooming a paw as if nothing were wrong.

"This is all your fault, cat!" He approached Alex menacingly. "Months ago, Seraphina gave you to me. A mangy little gift she offered so graciously. I should have known it was just a clever ruse to get her hands on some of my blueprints!"

Alex stopped grooming and sat up. He backed up slowly as the Clockwork Conqueror continued to advance.

"Hey!" Thimble squeaked from his hiding place. "Leave him alone!"

Suddenly he pushed over a large metal cog that had been leaned up against the wall.

A loud clatter echoed across the room.

Alex turned and hissed trying to warn his little friend to run.

The Conqueror's head snapped toward the sound.

"Who's there?"

Alex tried to rush between them but was too late as the mechanical arm shoved the pressure engine aside.

Thimble froze as the brass appendage loomed above. He tried to dart, but as the pressure engine shifted—the massive hand closed around him like a steel trap.

Alex trilled loudly begging his human to release Thimble.

"Thought you could stowaway, eh?" The Conqueror ignored the pleas and stared toward his workbench.

"Let me go!" Thimble shouted but all he heard was mere squeaks.

Alex desperately looked back and forth between the cruel man and his friend, trying to figure out how he could help.

His claws flexed against the floorboards. He was out of time—and no matter what he did, it might get Thimble hurt.

Alex made his decision. If he did nothing, it would almost certainly be the end of the little mouse.

With a furious yowl, he sprang forward, claws outstretched. He launched himself at the Conqueror's back, landing between the brass shoulder plates and sinking his teeth into the side of the man's neck.

The Clockwork Conqueror let out a howl of pain, staggering sideways. His grip on Thimble loosened—but only for a second.

"You miserable little beast!" he bellowed, clutching the mouse tighter and staggering toward the back wall where a row of small reinforced cages sat bolted to a steel shelf.

With a grunt, he shoved Thimble into the nearest one, slammed the door shut, and snapped the locking mechanism with a satisfying click.

Thimble squealed in protest, slamming his tiny body against the bars. "Let me out! Mister Alex! Help!"

Alex bit down harder and dug his claws deeper into the conqueror's neck.

"I hate cats," the Conqueror snarled. Reaching over his shoulder, he seized Alex by the scruff of the neck with his mechanical hand and peeled him off like a stubborn stain. Alex flailed, back claws raking against the man's coat, but they had no effect on the reinforced plating.

"Put me down!" Alex screeched, tail lashing violently.

Continuing to ignore his pleas, the Conqueror walked over to another cage, opened it with one hand, and shoved Alex inside with the other. The bars closed behind him with a harsh clang, and the lock snapped shut.

He stepped back, panting slightly, as his real hand closed around the back of his neck.

"Now," he muttered, glaring between them, "I don't know what kind of bond the two of you share but I won't have any more of this!"

He turned his back on them and walked toward his workbench, muttering to himself as he dressed his wound. After this, tools began to clink and gears began to whine.

"I don't have time to wait around on blueprints. I'm going to start my experiments here

Thimble was shoved into one cage
while Alex was forced into another one.

and now from memory."

He glanced towards Thimble's cage. The little white mouse backed away from the bars.

"You look like you wear an extra... extra... extra small."

At first, he only chuckled a little, then tipped his hat back and began to laugh maniacally. The sound was both jagged and eerie, as well as mechanical and sharp, rattling the tools on the bench.

CHAPTER XII

Where It All Comes Together

After spending numerous uneventful days stuck aboard the Aetherwind, on the evening of Thursday, October 27, 1881, Velvet stood on the deck and watched as the city of London sprawled below—glowing like a bed of embers beneath a velvet-black sky.

Lanterns lined the winding streets, and in the near distance, the spires of the British Museum pierced upward like watchful sentinels. Fog clung low to the rooftops, curling like steam from the earth itself.

Velvet balanced on the railing like a shadow, her sleek black fur ruffling in the breeze. The brass buckles of her leather vest caught the moonlight, and her little top hat sat smartly between her ears as she peered down at the glowing city below.

They were flying low now—too low for comfort if you asked Velvet—but Lady Blackwood seemed to have a purpose. The hum of the airship was muffled with stealth dampeners, and only the occasional flicker of brass plating gave them away in the dark.

"Hold our position here," Lady Blackwood said to the masked guard behind the helm. She stepped forward to the railing, cloak flapping in the wind.

Velvet's ears flicked. Her green eyes narrowed.

"*My humans*," she hissed under her breath, rising to all fours. Her gaze had locked onto a long shadow nestled in a quiet courtyard near the museum.

A silhouette too sleek to be mistaken for a rooftop. Angular. Familiar. It was the Phoenix.

"We made it," Velvet said. Her voice was low, but there was no mistaking the urgency in it.

"They made it." Blackwood's jaw tightened.

Velvet paced along the rail, paws soundless on the brass. "I've got to get down there to them!"

Seraphina wasn't paying her any attention. To her, it was just a small cat pacing back and forth restlessly. Lady Blackwood's gloved hand hovered over the compass at her side, though her eyes were fixed elsewhere.

Velvet followed her gaze and stilled.

A second airship moored some distance away in another secluded area.

Seraphina's voice dropped lower as she raised a spyglass and read aloud the name on the brass plate mounted to the side. "The Obsidian."

Velvet blinked as she looked up at the aristocratic woman.

"The Clockwork Conqueror's airship. That's how he's been transporting the members of the order here." Seraphina continued to speak aloud.

The Aetherwind circled the area a few more times before descending into a narrow clearing nestled between the Phoenix and the Obsidian. Fog swirled around the hull as they touched down.

Velvet's claws kneaded the rail. She had to get off this ship and onto the Phoenix somehow.

Lady Blackwood stepped back from the edge and signaled to her crew. "The four of you, stay here. Secure the ship. And make sure no one sneaks aboard."

Then, almost as an afterthought, she murmured to herself, "I'll take Tunnel Two. The northeast hidden entrance should still be clear and it leads directly to the holding cells."

She turned on her heel, cloak snapping behind her as she strode away down the gangplank, vanishing like a shadow in the night.

As Seraphina disappeared, Velvet slunk back across the deck of the Aetherwind, her movements silent as the moonlight. The fog off the Thames curled around the ship's mooring lines, cloaking the world in a thin, silvery veil.

The masked guards stood stationed near the

gangplank. Two remained on the ship near the top and the other patrolled the area in front.

She could wait and risk being stuck there the rest of her life or she could be clever and escape.

Choosing the latter, she crept low along the edge of the hull, using a coiled rope and a stack of tied-down crates for cover. Her vest brushed the deck with the faintest whisper of leather on metal. She crouched low and started padding her way to the loading ramp. She managed to slip past as they were keeping their attention high.

"Almost there..." She said to herself as she was halfway down the ramp.

"Freeze," one of the guards on the ground commanded.

The little cat immediately obeyed and froze.

The command from this guard immediately drew the attention of the guards still on the ship.

Defeated, Velvet turned and casually began to slink her way back up the ramp.

She had just reached the top when one of the guards unexpectedly scooped her up by the scruff of her vest.

"Intruder," he announced, glancing over his beak-shaped mask. "No one is allowed to sneak aboard."

And with an effortless swing, he chucked her off the side.

Velvet yowled—not out of fear, but outrage—as

she twisted in midair, tail flailing. She landed on all fours with a thump and a splash in the soggy grass below, barely missing a puddle.

She steadied herself, bore her teeth, and hissed, her hat skewed and one ear twitching furiously. "The nerve—!"

With a low growl, Velvet shook herself off and slinked into a grove of trees. "*Guess I should thank them for helping me off the ship.*" She thought, then shrugged it off as she took off running in the direction of the Phoenix.

She was about halfway there when she heard something terrifying.

A faint, metallic flutter—like gears turning inside wings.

Velvet ducked behind a large tree just as something landed behind her with a heavy thunk.

A low croak echoed in the night sky, strange and unnatural.

She turned, and there it stood: a clockwork crow, twice the size of a normal bird, with glowing crimson eyes and a beak polished to a razor sheen. Both of its wings clicked with every movement, and tiny gears turned along its spine.

Unlike the bird encountered earlier by Dottie, Panther, and Pat Bennington, this bird was completely automaton. Nothing about it was organic.

It sat there and studied her with its glowing red

eyes.

Slowly, it tilted its head, then without warning lunged at her.

Velvet dove aside as the crow's brass talons gouged into the dirt where she'd just been. She darted through the shadows, weaving between trees and shrubs, but the mechanical bird followed close behind. Its flight was jerky and angular, like a marionette pulled by invisible strings.

It shrieked. A high, ear-splitting battle cry *SKREEEEEEE.*

"I hate birds and I hate machines!" Velvet snarled, launching herself up the side of a tree, and clung to it by her claws. "But mechanical birds are the worst!"

The crow swooped in again, beak flashing like a blade.

And that's when it happened.

A sudden crack of blue-white electricity burst from the fog.

It barely missed the large metal bird by inches.

The cromatton, as Velvet would later name it, circled again and prepared for another attempt.

It was at this moment that a grey and white blur launched itself from the brush with a battle cry of its own.

It leaped into the air and tried to land on top of the winged monstrosity. But the creature banked hard and moved out of his way just in time.

"Alex!" Velvet trilled upon recognizing the older cat with the matching top hat.

The bird circled again and Alex prepared to pounce one more time. The little cat crouched low and then took off running as the cromatton started swooping in.

That's when Velvet noticed for the first time Alex's passenger. Thimble was riding high on his shoulders but he looked different. He was wearing some kind of metal armor suit.

Alex missed the attacker again by mere inches, but Thimble saw an opportunity and took it. He leaped off Alex's back and landed on the metal bird directly between its shoulders.

Blue-white electricity crackled through the air again as Thimble placed a metal rod against the side of its head. The crow jolted mid-air, shrieked once last time, and nose-dived to the ground into a twitching pile of cogs and metal feathers.

Velvet climbed down the tree, panting. Her fur stuck out in all directions.

A familiar squeaky voice echoed out from the wreckage of the mechanical bird.

"You looked like you could use some help."

Emerging from the fog, holding a still-crackling miniature Tesla rod, stood Thimble—his new armored suit gleaming in the moonlight. The gears in his chest whirred gently, and the copper plates around his ears made them look comically

Thimble was riding high on
Alex's shoulders, but he looked different.
He was wearing some kind of metal armor suit.

oversized—but heroic all the same.

Velvet stared.

"You look like a wind-up toy."

Thimble puffed his chest up inside his mechanical suit. "It's called the Rodent Avenger. And I just used it to save your whiskers!"

"You saved her?" Alex padded up beside the boastful little mouse. "You saved her, all by yourself?"

"We just saved her?"

"I'd like to think I helped." Alex meowed.

"I'm just glad you're both here." Velvet purred. "Never thought I'd see either of you again."

"I saw you when you landed," Thimble pointed in the direction of the Clockwork Conqueror's airship. "After I chewed through the cage Mister Alex was being held in we both made our way here as fast as we could. Oh, and my name isn't Thimble anymore. It's Sir Mousekerton now."

"You'll have to tell me all about it later," Velvet said, turning back in the general direction of the Phoenix. "And I'm not calling you that."

"How about Mechamouse?"

"Nope."

"Gizmo Mouse?"

"Forget it, Coppertail."

Thimble sighed but was too excited about his new suit to let it bring him down.

"Come on," Velvet said, her tone sharpening as

she looked toward the looming silhouette of the Phoenix.

"We've got to reach them—before it's too late."

The three little friends started down the path but Velvet suddenly stopped.

Her gaze turned to Thimble's suit—gleaming in the moonlight, all copper joints and tiny steam valves. Something about it…

A flash. A drawing.

The paper she hid under the bed when the man with the mechanical arm broke in.

"Wait," Velvet whispered. Her tail twitched sharply. "I've seen that suit before."

"My suit?" Thimble asked, standing a little taller.

"Not exactly. But close." Velvet turned to look back toward the Aetherwind, which was barely visible through the trees and fog. "A picture of one. We need to go back."

Alex groaned. "Of course we do."

Making a complete about-face, they set off again, moving swiftly but silently through the mist. Velvet took the lead, her black fur blending seamlessly with the shadows, while Alex padded behind her. This time, Thimble rode on Velvet's shoulders, hanging on to her vest.

As they neared the airship's mooring platform, movement caught Velvet's eye.

A strange noise started coming from the two

guards standing on the ground. They each pulled out wireless receivers from their coats and listened intently to the Morse code signal being transmitted. Then without saying a word, they turned and started towards the British Museum.

Meanwhile, the two guards remaining on the ship left their post and began to prepare for departure.

Velvet saw this as the perfect opportunity and didn't hesitate.

"We've got to act now!" she hissed as she dashed low across the clearing and up the ramp, with Alex on her heels. Not a sound except the faint hiss of steam escaping the stabilizers.

They slipped aboard unnoticed.

Velvet knew the Aetherwind like the back of her paw. She led them confidently across the deck straight to Seraphina's cabin.

They squeezed through the half-open doorway into the lavish private suite she knew so well.

While Alex looked around reminiscing about the time he had spent here, Velvet crouched low letting Thimble slide to the floor. After this, she crawled under the bed looking for the rolled-up paper.

A few seconds later, Velvet nosed her way back out.

"It's not here!" she hissed, tail lashing with frustration. "She must have moved it while I was taking one of my naps!"

Thimble looked up at her curiously and asked. "How many naps do you take?"

"I'm a cat." Velvet hissed in defense as she hopped onto the drafting table. "It's what we do!"

"*She wouldn't throw it away,*" Velvet murmured, half to herself.

Thimble leaned around her shoulder. "What did it look like again?"

"Paper," Velvet growled. "Pictures of animals wearing suits like yours!"

For the next thirty minutes, they searched the enormous room from top to bottom. Finally, in the back of Lady Blackwood's closet, Velvet found a large leather backpack hidden behind an ornate trunk. After managing to nose the flap open she spotted the blueprint she was searching for it was next to what was left of the schematics for the chronomechanism.

"Found them!" She meowed. "Just let me grab the one we came after with my teeth and we can get out of here!"

"Uh," Thimble suddenly interrupted, his ears twitching. "I hear footsteps and human voices."

Velvet pulled her face out of the satchel and raced to the large observatory window. The glass had been completely replaced after the Clockwork Conqueror had crashed through it days earlier.

She immediately spotted Lady Seraphina

Blackwood emerging from the shadows, followed by two masked guards and a group of weary-looking figures—prisoners by the look of them—one in a lab coat, others dressed plainly, their hands bound or restrained in some way.

"Take Thimble and hide!" Velvet ducked low. Alex rushed over, and Thimble scrambled onto his back. Without a word, the older cat bolted from the room, slipping into the shadows toward the cargo hold.

The two guards ushered the prisoners up the boarding ramp, guiding them below deck to some holding cells. The others were directed by Lady Blackwood to a couple of rooms on the same level as her private quarters.

Velvet hissed under her breath. There would be no escape now. Not with the guards so close and Seraphina bringing all these other humans on the ship.

Moments later, the Aetherwind gave a low mechanical whirrrr—then a hiss of pressure.

The deck shuddered.

They were lifting off.

"Oh no," Thimble whispered, peeking through the slats of the cargo bin. "We're trapped again!"

"Is that what's happening?" Alex snapped softly. "Because I thought we were about to be guests of honor at a banquet."

Back in the private suite, Velvet leaped up on

the middle of the settee and began grooming herself in an attempt to make everything seem normal.

As the ship rose into the London night, the lights of the city slowly shrank behind them. A low hum filled the air—the steady pulse of engines winding up to full cruising speed.

The Aetherwind soared into the sky, the Phoenix rising soon after.

****

Around seven o'clock the next morning, on Friday, October 28, 1881, the rocky outlines of an Island began to emerge through the mist.

Jagged cliffs and a shadowy tower loomed above the waves—ominous and waiting.

The Aetherwind glided lower, the thick fog parting as it began its slow descent toward Octopus Island. The cliffs rose like black teeth from the sea, half shrouded in mist and fog.

Velvet crouched at the cabin window, nose pressed to the glass. She moved around a little uncomfortable. Underneath her familiar vest she now wore a crisp white shirt that Lady Blackwood had put on her a few minutes prior.

"There they are," she whispered spotting the Phoenix as it came to a landing.

Down below, Alex padded over beside Thimble,

still peeking through a port hole in the cargo hold. They spotted the same thing.

Velvet's eyes narrowed.

"Somehow we've all got to get aboard that ship," she purred. "And I've got to bring those papers with us."

The ship gave a subtle lurch, and as the Aetherwind settled into place near the Phoenix, the wind howled past the glass like distant, mechanical laughter.

Lady Seraphina Blackwood reached inside her closet and picked up the leather backpack. She turned and met two of her guards on the deck of the ship along with a couple of the guests she had brought on board the night before.

"They're leaving," Alex whispered to Thimble as they peeked up the opening to the upper level.

They waited until the footsteps above faded, and were about to head up the ramp when Velvet suddenly appeared at the edge of the opening, silhouetted in the half-light. Her voice was barely audible.

"They're gone."

Alex gave a sharp nod. "Let's move."

The trio darted silently across the observation deck. They didn't speak as they crept toward the gangplank.

Quietly they slipped down it one at a time— Velvet first, then Alex with Thimble clinging to his shoulders. The remaining two guards didn't give them any trouble as they were watching the prisoners in the cells below.

The fog had grown thicker around Octopus Island, curling low across the path as though trying to keep them hidden.

Despite this, the three of them continued to keep low as they followed Seraphina, her guards, Jed, and the other humans.

Up ahead, the terrain shifted—winding paths gave way to a rocky clearing. Crumbling stone walls and rusted machinery cluttered the area.

Sometime later, Velvet slowed and ducked behind a boulder, gesturing for the others to do the same.

"Something's not right!" Velvet started sniffing the air. Her ears were laid back.

Alex started doing the same. "I smell it too!

Then came the hum.

It started low, like a tuning fork pressed to the earth, and built quickly into a pulsing thrum that made Velvet's fur bristle.

"What is that?" Thimble squeaked. "Let me at whatever it is! I'll take it on with my mechamouse suit!"

Velvet didn't answer. She couldn't. All three of them were staring in disbelief as the Clockwork Conqueror stepped from the shadows, moments later he flanked by two identical figures and three monstrous brass automatons.

"Still want to take them on..." Alex meowed then hissed, "Hey! Stop that!"

Thimble was trying to climb up on top of his head and hide under his hat.

Suddenly, the forest exploded into chaos.

Blinding light. A crackling boom. Sparks.

Lady Blackwood was almost hit but her two guards stepped in front of her taking the full brunt of the blast.

Alex ducked lower behind the rock. "That's it. We're done for. Back to the ship, now."

Velvet shook her head. "No."

Alex turned, ears flattening. "Are you insane? We just saw one of those things take out two guards like they were made of twigs!"

"I'm not going to fight," Velvet said, voice low but firm. "I'm going for what I came for." She nodded toward the satchel Seraphina had just removed from her shoulder and placed beside a large rock.

They all watched as Lady Blackwood drew two identical atomic blasters and joined the fight.

Thimble's mouth fell open. "You want to go into the middle of that battle?"

"No," Velvet replied. "I want to sneak into the bag while everyone's distracted."

"Nope," Alex hissed. "Absolutely, not."

"Sersaphina's busy fighting," Velvet pressed.

"She's not watching it. No one is. I can slip in and out again with those papers, while nobody is looking."

Alex opened his mouth but said nothing.

Thimble leaned around Alex's ear and asked. "We can't stop her, can we?"

"Not without tying her to a tree," Alex growled.

Velvet took a slow breath, steadying her nerves. Just ahead, the battle raged louder. Another beam of light scorched the ground. Voices shouted in total confusion. The whirr of clockwork limbs echoed through the clearing. She turned to the other cat.

"No matter what happens," she said, "take Thimble and get on the other airship. I'll meet you there if I can…"

Alex looked like he wanted to argue—but didn't. He just gave a single, sharp nod.

Velvet padded forward, low to the ground. Her top hat had been discarded somewhere along the trail. Her eyes gleamed with purpose.

She reached the satchel unnoticed, sniffed it once for certainty, and then pawed open the flap.

Just before ducking inside, she turned to them one last time.

"If this doesn't go as planned… say goodbye to Dottie and Panther for me."

For a heartbeat, she hesitated. Then flap closed and Velvet vanished.

The End for now...

A few days after the battle ended, golden light filtered through the slats of the barn at Davenport Ranch while dust motes danced like lazy fireflies in the air. Alex sat atop an overturned bucket, his front paws crossed like an old gunslinger waiting for a challenge. Thimble, still suited up in his Rodent Avenger armor, had climbed onto a bale of straw beside him, gesturing wildly as he reenacted the battle on Octopus Island—for the third time.

"And then, just as the second Conqueror raised his weapon," Thimble squeaked, striking a pose with his miniature Tesla rod, "Velvet looked back at Mister Alex and said, *take Thimble and get on the other airship. I'll meet you there if I can...*"

Panther was perched at the edge of the settee, eyes wide, claws kneading stuffing beneath him. His tail lashed in anticipation, every muscle taut like a coiled spring. Dottie sat next to the bale of hay, less dramatic but clearly listening, her ears perked. Alex sat in the background on one of the torn up arm chairs.

"What happened after she said *If this doesn't go as planned... say goodbye to Dottie and Panther for me?*" Panther blurted, leaning so far forward he nearly toppled over. "You said she got in the satchel, but then what? Did she make it out? Did she get caught? What happened next?!"

A quiet stillness settled over the barn. Even the wind seemed to hush.

Then—

A soft creak came from the door.

All four heads turned as a familiar silhouette appeared in the frame, haloed by the amber light of the setting sun.

Velvet trotted into the barn, a small feeding bowl with a looped handle swinging gently from her teeth, clinking with each step. Her top hat was neatly back in place. Her fur, though slightly ruffled, gleamed like polished coal.

She paused in the center of the room, set the bowl down with a dignified clink, and glanced up at Panther.

"We've already told you," she purred, "three times now."

"I know," Panther trilled. "But I just love hearing it!"

Thimble, still wearing his Rodent Avenger armor,
stood on the bale of hay and retold their
adventure, for the third time.

****

For those of you curious to know what happened to Velvet next, you'll have to read The Quest for the Lost Relic, an exciting Jedidiah Davenport Adventure story. Told from a human perspective, it intertwines with this story in the most purrfect way.

Want more adventures with the little black cat? Don't worry—Steampunk Velvet's journey has only just begun.

Prepare for more clever schemes, unexpected friendships, and daring escapes in The Further Adventures of Steampunk Velvet.

What secrets will she uncover next? What challenges will test her claws—and her courage?

Follow Velvet into her next thrilling adventure to find out!

And for those eager to return to the world of Jedidiah Davenport, don't miss the next volume in his continuing saga, The Mechanical Rebellion: A Jedidiah Davenport Adventure.

In this exciting tale, you'll finally meet the mysterious Brasswell—first hinted at in Steampunk Velvet.

Current titles in the
Steampunk Velvet Adventure Series

Current titles in the
Jedidiah Davenport Adventure Series

www.ingramcontent.com/pod-product-compliance
Lightning Source LLC
Chambersburg PA
CBHW050330110726
47899CB00007B/2443